OTHER YEARLING BOOKS YOU WILL ENJOY:

LONE STAR, *Barbara Barrie*
THE LION IN THE BOX, *Marguerite de Angeli*
OTHER BELLS FOR US TO RING, *Robert Cormier*
THE LITTLE WHITE HORSE, *Elizabeth Goudge*
CROCODILE CHRISTMAS, *Stephen Roos*
JOURNEY, *Patricia MacLachlan*
SHILOH, *Phyllis Reynolds Naylor*
NUMBER THE STARS, *Lois Lowry*
THE MORNING GLORY WAR, *Judy Glassman*
ARE YOU THERE GOD? IT'S ME, MARGARET., *Judy Blume*

YEARLING BOOKS/YOUNG YEARLINGS/YEARLING CLASSICS are designed especially to entertain and enlighten young people. Patricia Reilly Giff, consultant to this series, received her bachelor's degree from Marymount College and a master's degree in history from St. John's University. She holds a Professional Diploma in Reading and a Doctorate of Humane Letters from Hofstra University. She was a teacher and reading consultant for many years, and is the author of numerous books for young readers.

For a complete listing of all Yearling titles,
write to Dell Readers Service,
P.O. Box 1045,
South Holland, IL 60473.

THE CHRISTMAS REVOLUTION

Barbara Cohen

Illustrated by Diane deGroat

A Yearling Book

Published by
Dell Publishing
a division of
Bantam Doubleday Dell Publishing Group, Inc.
1540 Broadway
New York, New York 10036

The trademark Yearling® is registered in the U.S. Patent and Trademark Office.

The trademark Dell® is registered in the U.S. Patent and Trademark Office.

ISBN: 0-440-40871-7

Reprinted by arrangement with William Morrow & Co., Inc., on behalf of Lothrop, Lee & Shepard Books

Printed in the United States of America

October 1993

10 9 8 7 6 5 4 3 2 1

CWO

*For Frances Marshall
and the original Four Seasons:
Sara, Becky, Judy, and Harry.*

THE
CHRISTMAS
REVOLUTION

One

Emily Berg poked her twin sister on the arm. "Hey," she said, "this room looks na-ked."

Sally pointed to the bulletin board at the back of the fourth-grade classroom in Watch Mountain School. "You're not used to see-ing that board stripped bare," she said. "Mrs. Glendenning must be getting it ready for something special."

"More Christmas, I guess," Emily said.

Mrs. Glendenning had already hung little Santa Clauses from the shade pulls and a wreath on the classroom door. A fake tree waited in the back of the room for decorations. Christmas books were piled on the shelves in the library corner. Mrs. Glendenning was very big on holidays. She'd made a huge fuss over Halloween. They'd even celebrated Veterans' Day. And she'd started in on Christmas while a huge Thanksgiving turkey executed in colored chalks still decorated a corner blackboard. Emily thought it was too soon. She always felt a little funny when they started with Christmas in school. This year she was going to have to feel funny for a whole month.

She took her seat in the row by the windows. Sally sat in the row by the door. If there'd been more than one fourth grade in Watch Mountain School, Emily and Sally would have been in different rooms. Since there wasn't, seating them as far apart as possible was Mrs. Glendenning's compromise. She did this even though she was in no danger of mixing them up. Emily was fair and thin like their father; Sally was dark and plump like their mother. They were fraternal twins, not identical. They looked no more alike than any pair of sisters.

Being Sally's twin was all right with Emily—most of the time. She had the advantages of being a twin. She always had someone to play with. She did not have the disadvantages. Everyone knew who she was. No one ever called Sally Emily, or Emily Sally, except Grandma, who often ran through the entire list of her children, grandchildren, and dog before she managed to spit out the name she wanted.

Now and then Emily and Sally quarreled. But Emily fought a lot more with their older sister, Lisa, who was in eighth grade, than she did with Sally. Sally didn't fight with Lisa. Sally rarely fought with anyone. That was really the main trouble with Sally. She was perfect. Sometimes it was a pain to be Miss Perfect's twin.

The bell rang. Mrs. Glendenning called the class to order. The principal, Mrs. Titus, conducted the flag salute over the intercom. Then she read the announcements. After that came math and reading. Mrs. Glendenning believed in having the most important subjects first, while the kids were still fresh.

Mostly, Emily thought Mrs. Glendenning was pretty nice. She told them the reason for everything she did. And once, in assembly, the librarian had given Sally a box of pencils with her name on them for reading more books than any other student during the month of October. Afterward, Mrs. Glendenning had whispered to Emily, "If there were a prize for solving the most math problems correctly, you would have won it."

When Mrs. Glendenning had finished with all the reading groups, she took a roll of paper out of her desk drawer. "Boys and girls," she said, "look at this." She walked to the back of the room, unrolled the paper, and tacked it up across the top of the bulletin board. The paper was green. "Christmas Wishes," it said in large, elaborate red letters with sketches of trees, angels, and stars between and around them. "Take out your crayons," she ordered. "We're each going to draw a picture of what we want most for

Christmas. All of you, and me too. Then I'll hang the pictures up here on the bulletin board so your parents will be sure to see them when they come in next week for conferences."

"Are your parents coming in for a conference too, Mrs. Glendenning?" Petey called out.

Mrs. Glendenning smiled. "I don't know about my parents. They live far away, in Michigan. But I bet I can get Mr. Glendenning to stop by." She opened the closet door, took out a packet of drawing paper, and handed it to Tommy Andreotti, the paper monitor for the week. He started to pass it out.

Simeon Goldfarb raised his hand. Emily was surprised. Simeon always knew the answers when he was called on. But since he'd come to Watch Mountain, about a month after school had begun, he hadn't volunteered once. Unless he'd done it on one of the days Emily was out with the flu. Not very likely, she thought.

Mrs. Glendenning seemed surprised too

at seeing Simeon's hand, surprised and pleased. "Yes, Simeon," she said, still smiling.

Simeon stood up. Why did he do that? Emily wondered. Kids at Watch Mountain School didn't normally rise to their feet every time they were called on.

"I don't want anything for Christmas," Simeon said. "I don't celebrate Christmas."

"Oh, I know, Simeon, I know. You celebrate Hanukkah. You draw a picture of what you want for Hanukkah." She glanced from one twin to the other. "You too, Emily and Sally."

Before Simeon had come, the twins had been the only Jewish kids in the fourth grade. There were no more than a dozen others in the whole of Watch Mountain School. None of them were like Simeon, who pronounced his name Sim-eee-yun. Simeon wore a little cap on his head all the time. The other Jewish boys wore kipot on their heads only when they were in the synagogue or when they were doing something religious at home, like lighting the Sabbath candles. Most of the Jewish children in Watch Mountain, including Emily and Sally, went to religious school twice a week at Temple Brit Israel in New Hebron. But Simeon didn't go there. It wasn't traditional enough for his family.

Emily stared at Simeon. Everyone else was staring at him too. She wished with all her strength that he would sit down. Mrs. Glendenning had made a point of linking Emily and Sally with Simeon and Hanukkah. Most kids in the class thought Simeon was kind of weird. So did Emily. She didn't want to be connected with him.

But he did not sit down. He went on talking. "I don't get presents for Hanukkah."

"Why not?" Sally exclaimed.

"Are you very poor, Simeon?" Petey asked.

Simeon tossed his head. His crocheted kipah didn't fall off. It was held on with bobby pins. "We're not poor. My father gives my brother and me each a silver dollar every night of Hanukkah, when he lights the candles. I put the money in my bank."

"Well, maybe, Simeon, you would like something different this Hanukkah," Mrs.

Glendenning suggested gently. "That's what you can draw."

"Money is what you're supposed to get for Hanukkah," Simeon said. "Hanukkah *gelt*. Hanukkah money."

"Is that what you get, Sally, Emily?" Mrs. Glendenning asked. She sounded curious, as if she really wanted to know.

"We get presents," Emily said.

"One present each night," Sally added.

"Mostly they're little things, like doll clothes or a paperback book," Emily continued. "But there's always one big thing, one thing we really want."

"Then it's no problem for you two," Mrs. Glendenning said. She turned to Simeon. "Draw a picture of money if that's what you'd like to do. Or maybe you could draw a picture of something you hope for, like peace on earth. Everyone, no matter what their religion, hopes for peace on earth."

"I'll draw something," Simeon said, "but I don't want you to put it up on your Christmas bulletin board. I don't celebrate Christmas." And with that Simeon plopped down in his seat. It was clear he had uttered his last word on the subject.

"Very well," Mrs. Glendenning said quietly. "I will certainly respect your wishes."

Usually, before the class embarked upon an art project, the room was full of activity and conversation. But for once no one had a thing to say. No one moved either, except for Tommy Andreotti, who finished passing out the paper.

Emily leaned her head close to her desk and began to draw, as best she could, a picture of a ten-speed bicycle. Everyone else was drawing silently too, even Mrs. Glendenning, seated now at her own desk. But Emily found it difficult to concentrate on what she was doing. Her hands were sweating so much, she thought the color would come off her crayon and dye her palm purple.

Later, though, there was talk, plenty of talk, in the all-purpose room. Simeon wasn't there. He didn't take the bus to school each morning, like Emily, Sally, Petey, and Gloria. He lived just two blocks from the school and walked home for lunch.

Petey lifted the top piece of bread off her sandwich. "Yuch!" she exclaimed.

"What is it?" Emily asked.

"Peanut butter and marshmallow—I think," Petey replied. "I told my mother I *hate* peanut butter and marshmallow. But she doesn't believe me because it's what *she* likes."

"I'll trade you," Gloria said. "I have left-over chicken."

Petey pushed her sandwich toward Gloria. "Take it, and keep yours too." She rummaged in the bag and pulled out a package of potato chips. "I'm not hungry. This'll be enough for me."

"Thanks," Gloria said. That's how it happened most days. Gloria ate her own lunch and most of Petey's. Maybe, Emily thought, that was one reason why they were such good friends. They were like the couple in the nursery rhyme.

Jack Sprat would eat no fat,
His wife would eat no lean.
But between the two of them,
They licked the platter clean.

"I saw Mrs. Glendenning's picture on her desk when I went up to sharpen my pencil," Petey said. "She drew a dining-room table and six chairs. Isn't that a boring thing to want for Christmas?" She turned to Gloria. "What did you draw?"

"I drew a whole wardrobe of Barbie doll clothes."

"And you, Sally?"

"My own TV for my room, so I can watch what I want."

"I live in that room too," Emily reminded her.

"So we can both watch what we want," Sally amended.

"I want a ten-speed bike," Emily volunteered. "Dad says I'm too young, but I'm not. This town is nothing but hills. Even a two-year-old needs a ten-speed bike."

"At least you didn't draw silver dollars," Petey said. "Like Simeon. Simeon is weird."

No one disagreed.

"That little cap he always wears on his head," Petey continued. "That's really weird."

"It's called a kipah," Sally explained.

"Jewish men like my dad keep their heads covered when they pray, but really religious guys, like Simeon, keep their heads covered all the time."

"Even in bed?" Petey queried.

"Even in the bathtub?" Gloria wondered.

"Even on the toilet?" Petey asked with a giggle.

"How should we know?" Emily retorted sharply. "Ask him, if you're so curious."

"Boy, Emily," Petey said, "what're you so mad about?"

"I'm not mad." She took a long sip of milk, to cool off. "But don't ask me about Simeon. I don't know anything about Simeon."

"We just thought because you're Jewish . . ." Gloria's voice trailed off.

"We're not Orthodox. Don't think Sally and I are like Simeon. Because we're not."

"Of course you aren't," Petey agreed. "Simeon's *weird*."

After lunch on Mondays Mrs. Glendenning's class had music. Mr. Starrett was the music teacher. Short and round, he was wearing a plaid jacket and green pants. Put a beard on him, Emily thought, and he could pass for Santa Claus himself. "Our Winter Concert will take place in the all-purpose room Wednesday evening, December twenty-first, at seven-thirty," Mr. Starrett said. "I hope all your parents can come."

"December twenty-first is a very good day for a winter concert," said Mrs. Glendenning. "Does anyone know why?"

Several kids raised their hands. Mrs. Glendenning called on Gloria.

"It's the first day of winter," Gloria said.

"Very good, Gloria. The first full day of winter. If we sing in the winter, we won't mind the cold and the dark so much."

"We'll *carol* in the winter," Mr. Starrett said. "And we're going to start practicing for the concert right now." He placed a pile of songbooks on the first desk in each row. "Pass these back," he said. "You here in the fourth grade will sing, 'Winter Wonderland,' 'O Holy Night,' and 'Hark! the Herald Angels Sing,' plus the numbers the whole school is going to participate in. At the beginning everyone will do 'O Come, All Ye Faithful.' " Mr. Starrett stretched his arms wide. "The room will be dark, and you'll all come marching in with candles. Lit candles. Won't that be something?"

"We've never had lit candles before," said Mrs. Glendenning.

"Mrs. Titus got special permission from the fire department," Mr. Starrett explained. "And then, at the end, everyone will sing 'Silent Night.' The audience too." He glanced around the room. "Okay, you all have a Christmas songbook. Open to page twenty-two. We'll start with 'Hark! the Herald Angels Sing.' Really belt it out, kids. I'll be listening to you, very hard. I have to pick one of you to do the solo part in 'O Holy Night.' "

Emily glanced across the room. For a moment her eyes and Sally's locked. Emily knew what Sally was hoping. She was hoping Mr. Starrett would pick her. He probably would, too. Sally had the best voice in the fourth grade, maybe the best voice in all of Watch Mountain School.

Mr. Starrett blew a note on his pitch pipe. The class began to sing. While marking the rhythm with his waving hand, Mr. Starrett sang along, to keep them on key. But that didn't stop him from watching them. His eyes darted up and down the rows. Most of the kids weren't even looking into the songbook. They knew "Hark! the Herald Angels Sing" by heart. Emily certainly knew it. She'd been singing it every year since she'd entered kindergarten. She was sick of it, though she'd never said that to anyone, not even to Sally. All the other kids in the class seemed to love everything that went with Christmas as much as Mrs. Glendenning did.

Suddenly Mr. Starrett's hand fell to his side. He stopped singing. Everyone else stopped singing too. He walked down the aisle in the middle of the room. When he got to the next-to-the-last seat in the row, he paused. He gazed down at Simeon. "Young man," he said, "your mouth is closed. You cannot sing through a closed mouth."

"I don't sing Christmas carols," Simeon said. "My father and mother told me not to."

"Why?"

Emily felt her heart flop over inside her. She knew what would happen next. Simeon was going to do it again.

Simeon glanced down at the book of carols lying closed on his desk. Then he looked up again. "I'm Jewish. I don't celebrate Christmas."

"Oh." Mr. Starrett nodded. "I understand. But I have two Hanukkah songs in the program. The second grade is singing 'I Have a Little Dreidel,' and the sixth grade is singing a song in Hebrew, 'Sivivon Sov Sov Sov.' Here at Watch Mountain School we always have Hanukkah songs in our winter program."

The same two Hanukkah songs year after year, Emily thought. Not that she blamed Mr. Starrett for that. They sang the same few over and over again in Hebrew school too. There just weren't very many Hanukkah songs. Not nearly so many as there were Christmas songs.

"That doesn't make any difference, Mr. Starrett," Simeon said. "I still can't sing Christmas carols."

Now it was Mrs. Glendenning's turn.

"But if the other children, the children who aren't Jewish, can sing Hanukkah songs, why can't you sing Christmas songs?"

Simeon shook his head. "I can't."

"I don't understand," Mrs. Glendenning said quietly. "I think I'll call your mother. Perhaps if I explain to her that there are Hanukkah songs too—"

"You can call her," Simeon said. There was no emotion in his voice.

Mrs. Glendenning let out a deep breath. "For today you don't have to sing. You can do your math homework."

Simeon reached into his desk for his worksheet. He pushed the book of carols aside and bent over the paper. Mr. Starrett returned to the front of the room. Mrs. Glendenning sat down at her own desk.

"All right," Mr. Starrett said. " 'Hark! the Herald Angels Sing,' once more."

They sang the three songs about five times each. Emily was tired of them by the time the music period was over. She wondered if anyone else was.

Mr. Starrett conferred for a moment with Mrs. Glendenning. She smiled and nodded.

Then Mr. Starrett made his announcement. "I'm going to ask Sally Berg to sing the solo part in 'O Holy Night.' Will you do it, Sally?"

Sally's grin was so broad, Emily thought it might crack her face in two. "Yes, Mr. Starrett," Sally said. "Thank you."

"We'll rehearse your part next time. Meanwhile, you can practice at home yourself. You'll sing the first four lines alone, and then the rest of the class will join in."

Sally glanced down at her carol book. Emily looked at her own. "O Holy Night!" she read,

> . . . The stars are brightly shining,
> It is the night of our dear Saviour's
>   birth!
> Long lay the world in sin and error
>   pining,
> Till He appeared and the soul felt its
>   worth.

She had just sung those words, over and over again, without thinking about them much. But now, reading them, she realized they had meaning. When they sang "O Holy Night," they weren't just singing, "Tra la la." They were singing, "It is the night of our dear Saviour's birth." She knew what night the song was talking about. And she knew who the Saviour was supposed to be. Jesus. Jesus Christ. Well, he wasn't her saviour, and he wasn't Simeon's either. No wonder Simeon had shut his mouth. How could you sing those words while you were wearing a kipah on your head? It didn't make any sense.

On the bus going home, it was usually Sally who sat quiet and self-contained, while Emily, Petey, and Gloria fooled around. Today Emily stared silently out of the window, letting the others chatter. She was thinking about Simeon. He was weird, but he was brave too. Maybe you had to be a little weird to be so brave.

"I'm glad Mr. Starrett gave you the solo," Gloria said. "You have the best voice in the class."

"Thanks," Sally said. "But it's too bad he didn't make a few more solos, so some other kids would have a chance."

"I guess it's one solo per grade," Petey said.

"Well, it's too bad," Sally repeated. "Your voice is very nice too, Gloria."

"But it's not loud, like yours," Gloria replied.

"My mom told me," Petey said, "that when she was in fourth grade, she was a crow."

"You mean like a bird?" Sally questioned.

"Yeah. The teacher divided them into groups by ability, like we have reading groups, only these were singing groups. There were the nightingales and the robins and the crows. My mother was a crow."

"That's terrible," Sally said. "That's so mean."

"Teachers aren't so mean nowadays," Petey said.

Emily turned away from the window. "It was mean of Mr. Starrett to scold Simeon right in front of everyone for not singing."

"But he didn't know why Simeon wasn't singing," Sally said. "He stopped scolding when he found out why."

"I'm not going to sing Christmas carols

anymore," Emily announced suddenly, almost, but not quite, surprising herself. "You shouldn't sing them anymore either, Sally."

"But I have a solo!" Sally protested.

"You should give it up. You should tell Mr. Starrett you can't do it."

"For heaven's sake, why?" Sally's usually mild brown eyes blazed, and her cheeks turned bright red.

"Because we're Jewish too," Emily replied in a low voice. "We're just as Jewish as Simeon, even if we aren't Orthodox."

"Oh, Emily, don't be silly," Gloria cried. "You heard what Mrs. Glendenning said. If the Christian kids can sing Hanukkah songs, then the Jewish kids can sing Christmas songs."

"You know what I think?" Petey said. "I think you're jealous of Sally. I think you're jealous because she got the solo and you didn't."

"No!" Emily protested. "That's not it. That's not it at all." For the hundredth time, Emily thought how lucky she was that she and Sally weren't identical. Though of course if they had been, maybe Emily would have been a nightingale instead of a crow. Or maybe Sally would have been a crow instead of a nightingale.

Emily leaned back in her seat. Perhaps she was jealous—a little bit. But jealousy wasn't the main thing. "Sally can do what she wants," Emily said. "But I'm not singing any more Christmas carols."

"Weird," Petey said. "Weird. Just like Simeon."

Emily drew her lips together in a tight line. She wasn't like Simeon. Not in most ways. But she was like him in one way. She was Jewish. And she wasn't going to sing Christmas carols anymore. It would be uncomfortable not to sing them. But it had been equally uncomfortable to sing them. It had been uncomfortable all along.

Two

Grandma picked up Emily, Sally, and Lisa at four o'clock and drove them into New Hebron to do some Hanukkah shopping. She dropped them on Main Street. At six, when she closed her travel agency, their mother would drive them home.

They wandered through Grossman's Department Store, the bookstore, the hobby shop, the five and ten. They were looking for presents for two parents, three grandparents, and four close cousins. They didn't buy for all the other relatives. There were too many of them.

Every store was hung with tinsel, fir sprays, red ribbon, and colored lights. Grossman's windows depicted scenes from Santa's workshop. Elves lifted and lowered little hammers and saws. Reindeer shook their antlered heads and pawed the ground with their hooves. Mr. and Mrs. Santa loaded toys into sacks.

Their arms full of packages, the girls gazed silently at the display. Then they moved on, toward the Candy Kitchen, for something to drink. Each streetlamp along Main Street sported a real Christmas tree, decorated with lights. Loudspeakers had been suspended from storefronts at intervals, and Christmas carols could be heard from one end of Main Street to the other.

"Where are the Santas?" Sally asked. "There are always Santas on the corners, ringing bells and collecting money in kettles."

"It's too soon for them," Lisa explained.

"They don't usually show up until the week before Christmas."

"Their suits are all faded and moth-eaten," Emily said, "and their beards are scraggly. They look so phony. I mean, how can anyone in her right mind believe in Santa Claus? It's so dumb."

"What's gotten into you?" Lisa wondered. "Why are you so anti-Christmas all of a sudden?"

Before Emily could decide how to answer Lisa's question, Sally spoke. "Didn't she tell you? She's not going to sing Christmas carols this year. You know that Orthodox boy, Simeon Goldfarb, who came to our class in October? Today he told Mr. Starrett he wouldn't sing carols, and now Emily says she isn't going to sing them either."

Emily defended herself. "Sally's singing a solo. 'O Holy Night! The stars are brightly shining. It is the night of our dear Saviour's birth!' Do you think that's right? Do you think a Jewish girl should sing a solo like that?"

The wreath on the door of the Candy Kitchen was decorated with bells that tinkled as they opened the door and then closed it behind them. They sat at the counter, Emily in the middle. Lisa ordered a Diet 7-Up. The twins ordered hot chocolate with whipped cream. "If Sally has the best voice, she should sing the solo," Lisa said. "She doesn't have to believe the words. It's just a song."

"Sometimes I wish I lived in Israel," Emily said, "where most people are Jewish. Then I wouldn't have to worry about Christmas."

"Christmas is nice," Sally said. "We get off from school. The whole world is decorated. People seem happy. And I like the music. It's pretty."

"But Christmas makes me feel funny," Emily said. "Every TV show is about Christmas. Every ad is about Christmas. It's all over the place, except in our house. We don't celebrate it. The other kids talk about hanging stockings and going to church and pretending to their parents they still believe in Santa Claus. It makes me feel left out. It makes me feel different."

"If you don't sing carols with the rest of the class, you'll feel even more different," Sally pointed out. "You and Simeon not singing, and the whole rest of the class singing. Now *that's* different."

"I think you're confused," Lisa commented. "You'll get over it."

"Emily, you can do what you want," Sally announced firmly, "but don't drag me into it. I'm singing that solo, and that's all there is to that."

Emily didn't mention Christmas carols again, at least not that day. But the next afternoon, Mrs. Glendenning decided to have music again. Mr. Starrett came to the fourth grade only once a week. However, Mrs. Glendenning liked to sing too, so sometimes the fourth grade had a music period with her. "We'll practice our numbers for the Winter Concert," she said. "We'll try some other carols too, just for fun."

Emily raised her hand, and Mrs. Glendenning called on her. "Yes, Emily?"

"Can I speak to you for a minute?"

"How about after school?"

"It won't take long."

"All right."

Emily made her way to the front of the room. Mrs. Glendenning leaned toward her. "What is it?" she asked.

"I'm not going to sing Christmas carols," Emily replied softly. "I'm Jewish, and I'm not going to sing Christmas carols."

Mrs. Glendenning shook her head. "I don't understand." She turned toward the row by the door. "Sally, are you giving up Christmas carols too?"

Sally's eyes seemed hard as stones as she glanced in Emily's direction. "I am not," she announced firmly. "I don't see anything wrong with Christmas carols. They're beautiful."

Mrs. Glendenning smiled a little as she again faced Emily. "I'm going to teach the class one of the Hanukkah songs too," she said. "Won't that make it all right?" Emily felt her face turn red and her throat close. She couldn't speak. Instead, she clenched her fists and shook her head.

"If you don't sing the songs, you can't be in the Winter Concert," Mrs. Glendenning said.

Emily nodded. She understood that.

"All right," Mrs. Glendenning said. "You and Simeon, take some work with you and go to the library. I don't want you sitting here like two gloomy lumps on a log while the rest of us are trying to work up some Christmas spirit. Come back at one-forty-five."

Again Emily nodded. She returned to her desk and pulled out some worksheets. Simeon selected a couple of books, stood up, and walked toward the door. Emily followed. The classroom was silent. She was sure every pair of eyes was fixed on her back. She had to force her feet to take each step, because what they really wanted to do was run to her seat in the row by the window. But it was too late for that now.

Except for the aide, who was busy typing up cards for the catalog drawers, Emily and Simeon were alone in the library. They sat down at different tables and put their work in front of them. The room seemed very

warm. Emily stared at her papers. Then she put her head down on the table and shut her eyes.

"Why did you do it?" Emily sat up. Simeon was speaking to her. "Why did you do it?" he repeated. "You're not Orthodox."

"I'm a Jew," Emily responded tartly. "You don't have to be Orthodox to be a Jew."

"I bet you sang Christmas carols last year."

"A person can change her mind."

Simeon leaned forward. "Next Christmas I won't be here. In September they're sending me to a boarding school. A yeshiva. I'll only come home on weekends."

"A yeshiva's a Jewish school."

"Yes."

"I don't think I'd want to live away from home," Emily said thoughtfully. He'd volunteered a little information. She volunteered some in return. "I think I'm too young for that. Maybe next year I'll try summer camp for two weeks."

"I won't mind," Simeon said. "I'll have friends there."

"You could have friends here," she said.

"They knock off my kipah," Simeon said. "Whenever they get a chance."

"Who? The kids in our class?" Emily had never seen that happen.

"A couple of those big guys in the sixth grade. In the fall they did it, when we had recess on the playground."

"Oh, you mean guys like Rusty and Adam and Rod the Bod. They tease everyone."

"Before we moved here, we lived in Brooklyn. I went to a Jewish day school. Everyone there was Jewish." Simeon sounded wistful.

Emily picked up her worksheets and moved to Simeon's table. "What's it like at a Jewish day school?" she asked. "What do you learn there?"

"The same things we learn here. Reading, math, social studies. But other things too. Hebrew language, Bible, Jewish history. Every morning before school begins you have tefillot—prayers. Because there's so much to learn, you have to stay in school longer. Our school didn't let out until four o'clock."

"Yuch!" Emily exclaimed.

"But we didn't have to go to Hebrew school after regular school, like you do."

"Well, I don't like Hebrew school," Emily admitted. "But I'm not sure I'd want to go to regular school with only Jews either. I like being friends with Petey and Gloria." She remembered the conversation she'd had with her sisters at the Candy Kitchen the day before. Then she'd said she wanted to live in Israel. Now she was saying she didn't even want to go to a Jewish school. She was so confused, she felt as if her head was going to fall off. That's what the Christmas season did to a Jewish person. It messed up her brain.

Simeon stared at the book open on the table in front of him. "My best friend at my old school was Dov. We did everything together."

He sounded so sad. Until that moment

Emily had been convinced that he had no friends at Watch Mountain because he didn't want any. She wasn't so sure anymore. "Listen, Simeon," she said, "you want to come to our family Hanukkah party? After the presents we have a big dinner and a play. It's a lot of fun. All my cousins come. Jake is in third grade and Chip is in the seventh. Maybe you'd like to meet them."

He looked up at her. "Your parents won't mind?"

"It's at my grandmother's," Emily explained. "I'm absolutely sure she won't mind."

"I'll ask my mother," Simeon said. "I'll let you know."

Emily nodded. Once again her mouth had spoken before her brain had had a chance to think of the consequences. She had told the truth when she'd said her grandmother wouldn't mind. Grandma was the most hospitable human being on earth. Whenever one of her grandchildren asked if they could bring a friend to her house, she always said, "What's a home for if not to fill up with people?"

But Emily wasn't so sure how her sisters and cousins would react. How would they feel about being nice to a weirdo at their Hanukkah party? Of course, he wasn't *very* weird. Only a little weird. Emily knew that now. But she was the only one who knew.

Simeon glanced at the clock. "I think it's time for us to go back," he said. They picked up their books and papers. Side by side they marched down the hall to the fourth-grade room.

The social-studies lesson had already begun. Petey was reading out loud from the history book about the causes of the War of 1812. Emily and Simeon slipped quietly into their seats. No one spoke to them; no one seemed to notice them, not even Mrs. Glendenning.

Later, on the bus, Petey and Gloria started talking about Christmas shopping. "I've saved up twenty-seven dollars and thirty-eight cents," Petey said. "I hope it'll be enough. I have so many presents to buy."

"Listen, Petey," Gloria responded, "don't buy for me this year, and I won't buy for you. We'll save a couple of bucks that way."

"You know what you could do?" Emily, sitting next to the window, leaned across Sally. "You could make cards and send them to each other. That wouldn't cost anything, but you'd still be remembering each other—you know what I mean?"

Petey went right on talking. She acted as if Emily hadn't said a word at all. "Well, Gloria," she said, "I don't think that's such a hot idea. Who's more important to me than you? Who's more important to you than me?" She reached across the aisle and put her hand on Sally's arm. "Right, Sally?"

"Don't mix me up in this," Sally said with a laugh.

Did Sally realize that Petey was ignoring Emily? And why was Petey ignoring her? It was not a question Emily could ask, not now, not on the bus. Petey must have decided Emily was just as weird as Simeon. Emily pretended she hadn't noticed she'd been cut out of the conversation. She turned away and stared out the window.

Afterward, driving to Hebrew school in the car pool, she asked Sally about it. "Did you notice?" she said. "Did you notice that going home on the bus Petey wouldn't speak to me? Neither would Gloria. I said something and they ignored it."

"Oh, you're imagining things," Sally said. "You're too sensitive, Emily. You think everyone's out to get you."

"We'll see," Emily said darkly. "We'll see what happens tomorrow."

Mom drove the Hebrew-school car pool home. She told Emily and Sally to set the table as soon as the three of them walked into the house. Lisa cut up fruit for dessert. Dad made the salad. It was Mom's turn to prepare the main course. She served the beef stew that had been cooking in the Crockpot since early that morning. Then she sat down next to Dad. "I got an unexpected call at the office this afternoon," she said. "From Mrs. Glendenning."

"Mrs. Glendenning?" Emily and Sally both spoke at the same time.

Mother picked up her fork. "There was something she wanted to talk about, something she didn't understand."

"Like what?" Emily asked, though she already had a pretty good idea.

"Like why you won't sing in the Winter Concert." Mother speared a piece of potato and popped it into her mouth.

"Emily has decided not to sing Christmas carols," Sally said. "She's decided she's too Jewish to sing Christmas carols. She wants to be like Simeon Goldfarb."

"I do not!" Emily protested. "You shut up, Sally. I can explain myself."

"Well, I wish you had mentioned your decision to us," Dad said. "It would have been nice to hear about it from you, instead of from Mrs. Glendenning."

Emily pushed at a piece of meat with her fork. "I was going to tell you. I mean, I just started not singing today." Then she looked up at her father. "Do you think there's anything wrong with it?"

Slowly, her father shook his head. "No. I don't think you should sing Christmas carols if you don't want to. I guess I'm just kind of surprised that you don't want to." He smiled a little, as if remembering something. "You know, when I was a little boy, I wanted a Christmas tree more than anything. I knew we were Jewish, but I really didn't understand why we couldn't have one. They were so beautiful, and they didn't have crosses on them or anything like that. One year, after the holidays were over, I dragged a discarded tree home from someone's garbage heap and set it up behind the garage. It was still covered with tinsel. It stood there until my father found it when he was cleaning up the yard in the spring."

"Was he mad at you?" Lisa asked.

"No," Dad said. "By that time it had lost the tinsel and all its needles too. It was just a skeleton. He didn't know where it had come from. He didn't realize it was a Christmas tree, and I never told him."

"I never wanted a Christmas tree when I was a little girl," Mother said. "I think your dad wanted one because his family never celebrated the Jewish holidays. They didn't celebrate *any* holidays. But you know Grandma and Grandpa. When I was a little girl, they had two seders for Passover, and a family dinner before Rosh Hashana, and a break-the-fast after Yom Kippur, and a big Hanukkah party, just the way they do now. So I didn't miss a Christmas tree."

"Did you sing Christmas carols in school?" Emily asked.

Her mother and father both nodded. "In those days we did what our teachers told us to do," Mother said. "We didn't make waves. I said the Lord's Prayer every morning too, even though Jesus wrote it. They don't make you say the Lord's Prayer anymore."

"It never occurred to me not to sing them," Dad said. "I never thought of it."

Mother turned and gazed at Emily. "Like Dad, I wish you'd told us about this before Mrs. Glendenning did. But I want you to know I'm proud of you, Emily. I think you're doing a very brave thing. I'm behind you, and that's what I'm going to tell Mrs. Glendenning."

"But what about me?" Sally exclaimed. "I have a solo. Emily thinks I should give it up." She slammed her knife down on the table. "But I don't."

"You don't have to." Her father patted her arm gently. "We're proud of you, too. We'll burst our buttons when you sing that solo at the Winter Concert."

Lisa's eyes rested first on one twin and then on the other. "You know," she said, "once in a while I've wished there were two of me, like there are of you. Then I'd get lots of attention, and I'd never be lonesome. But I guess having your twin sister in your class sometimes can cause a little trouble."

A little trouble, Emily thought. A little trouble? It seemed like big trouble to her. Sally wasn't the cause, but she was part of it. Emily remembered sitting in the library with no one but Simeon. She remembered Petey and Gloria ignoring her on the bus. And now Sally was cross with her too. She had the uncomfortable feeling down in the pit of her stomach that the trouble was going to get a lot worse before it got better.

Three

The fourth grade made paper chains to decorate the huge school Christmas tree that stood in the hall in front of the main office. Emily made them too. Even Simeon made them. Emily supposed it was all right to make paper chains. In themselves, they had nothing to do with Christmas.

Each class made something for the tree. The sixth graders produced angels. They used white construction paper for the faces and robes, yellow yarn for the hair, and gold wire for the wings and halos. The fifth graders baked gingerbread people. Emily decided they were the luckiest. They prepared more gingerbread than they needed and ate what was left over. She hoped they would be assigned gingerbread people next year too, when she was a fifth grader. The third graders wrapped empty boxes in brightly colored paper to look like presents under the tree, waiting to be opened Christmas morning. The second grade made stars out of foil—not just silver foil, but red and green and gold foil too. The first grade strung popcorn. They also got to eat leftovers. Even the kindergartners had a job. They colored and cut out red-and-white-striped candy canes and stockings.

Two kids from each class were allowed to help Mrs. Titus and the custodian, Mr. Oliver, hang the decorations on the tree. "You're all wonderful boys and girls," Mrs. Glendenning said. "Every one of you deserves to help trim the tree. But since we can't all go, I'll choose two of you by lot." She put folded slips of paper, on which she'd written the names of the students, into a shoe box. The new paper monitor was Melody Mopcik. Mrs. Glendenning asked her to shut her eyes and pull out two of the slips.

Emily glanced at Simeon. His eyes were fixed on Melody, his lips drawn together in a thin line. She knew what he was thinking—the same thing she was thinking. What would happen if her name was drawn? Would she help decorate the Christmas tree? Was decorating a Christmas tree the same as singing carols? There were stars on it, and angels. Emily knew that the stars represented the super-bright one that the New Testament said shone over Bethlehem the night Jesus was born. According to the story, angels too had attended his birth. Even though her class had made only paper chains, would it be right for her to decorate a tree with angels and stars on it?

Melody pulled out a slip and handed it to Mrs. Glendenning. The teacher unfolded it and read out the name. "Tommy Andreotti," she said. Melody pulled another slip. "Petey Haberman," Mrs. Glendenning said.

Emily relaxed. Glancing once again at Simeon, she saw him lean back in his seat too.

Later, when they were in the library together during music period, she asked him what he would have done if his name had been picked.

"I wouldn't have gone," he said. "What would you have done?"

"I don't know," she admitted. "I'm not sure putting paper chains on the tree is the same as singing 'O Holy Night.' "

"Yes, it's the same," he said. "For me, it's the same."

"You know," she remarked thoughtfully, "maybe our names weren't even in the box. Maybe knowing how we feel about the carols, Mrs. Glendenning just left our names out."

"Possible," Simeon said. "I didn't think she was that smart."

"Mrs. Glendenning is very smart," Emily exclaimed. "I like her a lot."

"Well, she's all right, I guess." Simeon didn't sound so sure.

"Can you only like Jews?" Emily wondered. "Is that one of the rules of being Orthodox?"

"Of course not!" Simeon retorted. "That's a lousy thing to say." He turned away and opened the book he was reading. It was one of the Great Brain's adventures. Emily had read some of those books. The Great Brain wasn't Jewish. He lived in Utah.

"I'm sorry," Emily said. "I wasn't trying to be mean."

He spoke without looking up from the table. "My mom said I could come to your Hanukkah party, but now I'm not so sure I want to."

"Oh, Simeon, I said I was sorry. Sometimes things just come out of my mouth. Sometimes I just don't think." This time it was Emily who glanced up at the clock. "Maybe it's time to go back to class," she suggested.

They had to pass the main office to get to the fourth-grade room. Mr. Oliver had strung the lights, and now, on a ladder, he was adding the final touch to the tree; a huge, glittery, three-dimensional star constructed by the art teacher. He placed it on the topmost branch. It brushed against the ceiling. Tommy, Petey, and the other decorators stood back, admiring their handiwork.

"Hi, Emily," Tommy called out. "Hi, Simeon." Petey turned, but she didn't say anything. Emily and Simeon stopped walking and gazed at the tree.

"It's really pretty," Tommy said.

"Pretty?" Petey snorted. "It isn't pretty. It's beautiful. Isn't it?"

"Yes," Emily agreed. "It's beautiful."

Petey stared at Simeon. "Don't you think it's beautiful?"

Simeon said nothing.

"Are you an American?" Petey asked sharply.

"Yes," Simeon said. "Of course."

"Christmas is an American holiday," Petey snapped. "Everyone celebrates it."

For a moment she and Simeon glared at each other. Then Simeon turned to Emily. "You coming?" he asked.

"I'll be along in a minute," Emily said. "I

just want to look at the tree a little longer."

Simeon started down the hall again. Petey stared at Emily. "Oh, go on," she said. "Go with your boyfriend."

Emily stepped back. "He's *not* my boyfriend," she protested.

But Petey was no longer listening. She was bending down to pick up one of the paper chains that had fallen off the tree. Then she stood up and carefully looped it over a branch.

Emily once again began moving down the corridor toward the fourth-grade room. She didn't rush to catch up with Simeon. He was several yards ahead of her. Petey was behind her, still absorbed in the tree. Emily walked alone.

That afternoon, when school was dismissed, the whole class filed by the tree on their way out of the building. It was the first time that most of them had seen it decorated. "Oh, it's gorgeous," Melody Mopcik said. "It's the best tree we've ever had."

Gloria agreed. "It's better than the tree we have at home. That's because it's so much bigger, and because it's real. Our tree is made out of plastic."

"Simeon doesn't think we should have a tree," Petey announced in a loud voice. "Isn't that right, Simeon?"

Simeon's eyes narrowed. "My father says religious symbols don't belong in public schools."

"My father says . . . my father says . . . my father says," Petey repeated. Some of the kids around her joined in the chant. "My father says . . . my father says . . . my father says . . ."

Simeon made no reply. He marched forward, his eyes on the door. He pushed it open and hurried down the steps, down the walk, and across the street. Petey stood on the curb. "My father says . . . my father says . . . my father says . . ." she called out. But Simeon didn't turn around. He acted as if he didn't even hear her. Emily watched him go.

Petey climbed on the bus. Emily was behind her. "Your boyfriend's a spoilsport," Petey said.

"I told you, he's not my boyfriend."

"He's a spoilsport anyway. I hate him." And that was the last thing Petey said to Emily the whole ride home.

The Christmas tree stood tall, glittering, and graciously welcoming in the front hall at Watch Mountain School. Everyone entering the building over the next three days stopped to gaze at it. Some parents, picking up their kids after school, made a point of coming inside just to see it. That wasn't really necessary. The tree would still be there the night of the Winter Concert. Then every mother and father would have a chance to admire it. Also brothers, sisters, grandmothers, grandfathers, aunts, uncles, cousins, and friends. At least, that's how it had been other years.

On a miserable, sleety Thursday morning, Emily and Sally and all the other kids on their bus clattered up the stairs of the school building and pushed their way through the front door. They found Mrs. Titus in the hall, and Mrs. Glendenning, and most of the other teachers. Mr. Oliver was there too. So was Simeon, standing by the door to the main office. He took a hesitant step toward Emily. Every face in the corridor was as long as a basset hound's. Mr. Oliver shook his head. Mrs. Titus, who weighed about 250 pounds, was panting. Mrs. Glendenning wiped a tear from her cheek.

The tree was on the floor. It stretched from the office past the first-grade classroom and halfway to the second-grade classroom. Little pieces of glass glittered among the pine needles that now carpeted the tiles. Crushed angels, torn chains, bent stars, and creased candy canes clung to branches at crazy angles or lay scattered about on the ground. Strings of popcorn had broken, and with every step Emily felt a white puffy kernel crunch under her shoe. Water from the stand, which was also lying on its side, had soaked some of the stockings and other paper decorations all the way through.

"All that work!" Tommy Andreotti exclaimed. "All that work for nothing."

Now that the hall was full of kids, Mrs. Titus recovered her voice. "Students, teachers, go to your classrooms. Right now. Mr. Oliver and I will get to the bottom of this. But we can't do anything with all of you milling around in the corridor."

Mrs. Glendenning took the lead. "Tommy," she called, "Sally, Emily, Petey, Gloria, Simeon, come along now." She turned around and started down the hall. Some of the other teachers began calling out names. Clumps of students followed their teachers. Slowly, the mob evaporated. Mrs. Titus remained by the door, shooing kids to class as they came in from the buses. Mr. Oliver began the business of cleaning up.

In the fourth-grade room it was a long time before the class got down to work. They wouldn't be able to concentrate on learning anything until they'd gotten all their questions and opinions about the fallen tree out of the way. Mrs. Glendenning knew that. She let them talk.

"Was the tree too heavy?" Tommy asked. "Is that why it toppled?"

"Yes," Gloria said. Her voice was hardly more than a whisper. "That's why it fell.

I'm sure that's why. It toppled over all by itself."

"Except for the star, all it had on it was paper, gingerbread, popcorn, and a few strings of lights," Petey retorted. "Those things aren't heavy. They'd never make a big tree like that fall over."

"Maybe there was an earthquake," Melody suggested thoughtfully. "One that we couldn't feel but the tree could."

Petey pooh-poohed that suggestion. "This isn't California. If we didn't even feel this earthquake, how could it knock over a tree five times bigger and heavier than any of us? And how come the tree here in our classroom stood up just fine? It's a lot smaller and a lot lighter than the one in the hall. It doesn't even have any decorations on it yet."

"So Petey, what *do* you think happened?" Melody asked.

"Someone knocked that tree over. I'm sure of that." Petey spoke with absolute conviction.

"Someone accidentally ran into a tree as big as that one?" Tommy responded scornfully. "That seems about as likely as Melody's earthquake."

Petey replied slowly, in a low, mysterious voice. "That tree was *knocked* over," she said. "It was knocked over *on purpose*."

Gloria stared at Petey, wide-eyed.

"Oh, Petey!" Sally exclaimed. "Who would do a thing like that on purpose?"

"Someone who doesn't have to take a bus," Petey said. She wasn't looking at Sally, who'd asked her the question. She was looking at Simeon. "Someone who could get here before any of the other kids, before the teachers even. Someone who could get here before everyone, except maybe Mr. Oliver. And while Mr. Oliver was down in the basement, checking the boiler, or out front, hanging out the flag, this person could rush in the front door, knock over the tree, and rush out again." She turned around, and leaned back in her seat, looking as satisfied as a detective who'd just solved a murder.

"But why?" Sally asked. "Why would anyone *want* to knock over the tree?"

Petey raised her eyebrows. "Your sister might know that better than me. I think it would have to be someone who hates Christmas." Again she swiveled around in her seat and looked at Simeon. He didn't look back at her, but he didn't look down at his desk top either. He stared straight ahead, as if he hadn't heard one single word of the conversation.

Emily wished she hadn't heard it. She wished her hands had been over her ears. She knew, as surely as she knew her own name, that if she hadn't ridden the same bus to school as Petey Haberman, Petey would have accused her of being Simeon's partner in crime.

Mrs. Glendenning walked across the room so that she was standing in front of Petey's desk. "You know something, Petra Haberman?" she said.

Petey looked up, her eyes wide. No one in the class, not even Mrs. Glendenning, had ever yet called her Petra.

"It's very foolish to accuse someone of something," Mrs. Glendenning continued, "unless you're absolutely sure he or she did it. Unless you have proof. Are you accusing someone, Petra?"

Petey's eyes fell, and so did her voice. "No," she mumbled.

"What was that?" Mrs. Glendenning asked.

"No, Mrs. Glendenning," Petey repeated.

"That's good," Mrs. Glendenning said. She lifted her head and spoke to the whole class. "Let's get started around here. It's time for math. Melody, pass the worksheets on my desk out to the class. When I find out more about the tree from Mrs. Titus, I'll let you know. Meanwhile, we have to get something done. We can't waste the whole day."

The morning passed. There was no more public discussion of the fallen Christmas tree, but there was plenty of murmuring. It swirled around Emily like leaves around her feet on a windy autumn day. But no one said a word to her about it. As a matter of fact, no one said a word to her about anything.

At lunch she ate, as usual, with Sally, Petey, and Gloria. Except for occasional nasty remarks, Petey and Gloria had pretty much ignored Emily since she had stopped singing Christmas carols. But they all continued to sit at the same lunch table. Petey and Gloria weren't mad at Sally. And where else would Emily sit, if not at the table with her own sister?

"When I took that note to Miss Westervelt's room, I had to pass the main office," Petey said. "The hall there is all cleaned up."

"Where's the tree?" Sally asked.

"It's standing back up again. It looks a little skimpier. That's because it lost a few of its branches. And of course it has no decorations."

"I guess we'll have to make them all over again," Sally said.

"What's the use?" Petey said. "He'll just knock the tree over again. Right, Gloria?"

Gloria said nothing. She just kept on eating.

But Emily could contain herself no longer. "Who's *he*?" she exclaimed.

Petey stared at her for a long, slow moment before replying. "I think you know."

"Do I? I want to hear you say it."

"Simeon." Petey spit out his name as if it were a toad. "Simeon Goldfarb. Your boyfriend."

"He's not my boyfriend," Emily protested. "I told you that."

"He's not." Sally rushed to her defense. "We hardly know him."

"Maybe *you* hardly know him," Petey said, "but *she* knows him. She sits with him in the library during singing three or four days a week." Petey turned to Emily again. "Has he kissed you, Emily? Has he kissed you in the library? I bet his breath stinks and his lips are all wet and oogy."

"Oh, Petey, shut up," Emily cried.

"Remember what Mrs. Glendenning said," Sally interjected. "Don't accuse someone unless you have proof."

"There'll never be any proof," Petey said. "I never said Simeon was dumb. He's a creep, but he isn't dumb. He certainly wasn't going to knock over the tree while someone was watching, so how can there ever be proof?"

"Well, then, just drop it," Sally insisted.

"I won't," Petey shot back. "Why should I? He did a terrible thing. I want him to know he can't get away with it."

"Listen, Petey," Emily said, "he wouldn't do that. I know he wouldn't. He just isn't that kind of person."

"Well, naturally, *you* have to say that," Petey returned.

"Well, it's true." Emily stretched her hand across the table in her sister's direction. "Isn't it, Sally?"

"I think so," Sally said. "I don't know him at all, but I think so."

"Well, maybe you have to say that too," Petey returned.

"Look, Petey, I haven't got anything against Christmas," Sally said. "Remember?"

"Yeah, I remember. The solo."

Suddenly Gloria spoke. "Hey, Petey, what kind of sandwich do you have? You want to trade?" It seemed as if she was trying to change the subject.

"Muenster cheese and jelly," Petey said. "Yuch. You can just have it. And then you can come over to my house after school and eat up every bit of Muenster cheese and every bit of grape jelly in the house so I don't have to look at them again."

Gloria held the sandwich in front of her face and stared at it. "Your mother will just buy some more."

"Not for a few days."

Emily and Sally locked glances. Emily knew they were thinking the same thought. A week ago, Petey would have asked the twins to come over too. But not this time.

When lunch was over, Emily and Sally walked out of the all-purpose room side by side. Petey and Gloria had disappeared up the stairs. "Now Petey isn't our friend anymore," Sally said. "So Gloria won't be either. Because whatever Petey does, Gloria does too."

"Petey hasn't been my friend for days and days," Emily said.

"Maybe she'll get over it after Christmas," Sally offered hopefully.

"I don't care if she does," Emily retorted. "I don't want to be her friend. She's turned into someone very mean."

Suddenly, Sally stopped walking, forcing Emily to stop too. "You know what?" Sally said. "You don't care if we end up without any friends at all."

"Of course I care," Emily returned.

"Then why did you get involved in this whole Christmas revolution?" Sally wanted to know. "It's all right for Simeon. He didn't have any friends to start with. But look what you've done to yourself. Now you've done it to me, too. They're leaving me out now just because I'm your twin."

A dark thought occurred to Emily. "Maybe just because you're Jewish," she countered. It was something she would have expected Simeon Goldfarb to say, not herself, not Emily Berg.

"Don't be silly," Sally said. "They've known us since kindergarten. Since before. Since nursery school."

"Go catch up with them," Emily urged. "Tell them you'll come over to Petey's house this afternoon by yourself. Maybe they'll let you." That would be a test.

Sally sighed. "You know I can't go without you."

Emily nodded. It was their way. No matter how mad they got at each other, they always stood together against the rest of the world. Sally might scold Emily about the way she kept her side of the room. Or she might get annoyed with Emily when she wanted to read and Emily wanted to play. Or she might complain about Emily to Lisa, or to Mom and Dad. But she'd never say a word against Emily to anyone else. And vice versa, of course.

Four

Aunt Lou drove Emily, Sally, Jake, and
Jenny to Hebrew school at quarter to four
and picked them up again at six. Then she
dropped them off at Aunt Nan's house for a
meeting of their cousins' club, the Four Seasons. The twins' mother or father would
take all of them home at nine o'clock. "If
we'd been invited to Petey's this afternoon,
I guess we'd have had to turn her down
anyway," Sally pointed out as they made

their way up the walk in front of Aunt Nan's condo. "We wouldn't have been able to stay more than five minutes, on account of Hebrew school."

The club had been Aunt Nan's idea. Actually she was their great-aunt, their grandmother's sister. She lived alone and worked as an office manager for a chemical company. Emily knew that she and her sisters and their four cousins were Aunt Nan's favorite people in all the world. Relatives who had children of their own couldn't care about a person exactly the way Aunt Nan did. Your parents certainly couldn't. It was their job to make you shape up. All Aunt Nan had to do was love you.

The Four Seasons had dinner at Aunt Nan's house about once a month, more often if they were planning a production. She made all the things kids like best—hamburgers with gooey toppings, spaghetti and meat balls, tuna fish and noodles baked in big sea shells, chocolate cake. But she served these things to them with sterling silver on Limoges china and a linen cloth, as if they were grown-ups. She always had flowers in the middle of the table.

"Billy Carstairs says Simeon Goldfarb knocked over the tree," Jenny said as she pushed Aunt Nan's doorbell. "Billy said that's what Petey told him."

"I heard that too," Jake added. "I heard it from Petey's brother Ralphie."

Cripes, Emily thought. If Petey had spread that story to the fifth and the third grades, it was probably all over the first, second, and sixth grades too. Probably even the kindergartners had heard it.

Aunt Nan was opening the door. "It's not true," Emily said. "I know it's not true."

"Hello, darlings," Aunt Nan said. "What's not true?"

"Simeon did not knock over the Christmas tree." They were in the vestibule now, taking off their coats and hanging them in the closet.

"How do you know he didn't?" Jenny asked.

"How does Petey know he did?" Emily retorted. "Listen, I know Simeon better than

Petey does, and I know he wouldn't do a thing like that. I just know, that's all."

"What Christmas tree are you talking about?" Aunt Nan queried as she led them to the table. They usually ate as soon as they showed up. First of all, they arrived hungry. Second of all, the smells in the apartment were irresistible. And third of all, tonight they had to leave plenty of time to practice.

Aunt Nan served the meal. It was fried chicken and mashed potatoes. Between mouthfuls, they told her about Sally's solo, Emily's refusal to sing carols at all, the tumbled-down Christmas tree, and Simeon's leading role in the Christmas revolution.

"I'm coming to the Winter Concert," Aunt Nan said. "I certainly want to hear that solo."

"Jake and I will be singing too," Jenny said, "even though we don't have solos."

"Yes, I know," Aunt Nan returned. "I want to hear you, too, and see you. The Winter Concert is always a lot of fun."

"I hate it," Jake said. "I hate singing. I

think I'm going to join Emily and Simeon's revolution."

"Hating singing is not a good reason," Emily said.

"No one will know it's my reason," Jake countered. "I'm just as Jewish as you are."

Emily said no more. Let Jake join the revolution for his own reasons, whatever they were. She and Simeon could use any support they could get. She'd rather the new recruit were a sixth grader, but even a third grader was better than no one.

"At least you two will be in the play we're doing for the family Hanukkah party," Aunt Nan said. "That'll make up a little bit for not being in the Winter Concert."

"I don't want to be in the Hanukkah play either," Jake said. "It's really dumb, dressing up in bathrobes with towels on our heads and aluminum-foil swords."

"But Jake!" Aunt Nan was shocked. "You have to be in the play. We can't do the play with just the girls. It's a Four Seasons play. You have to be in it."

Jake waved his drumstick. "I only come

here for the food. The club is silly too. What am I doing in this club? I'm going to resign." Though he was only in third grade, Jake knew words like "resign" because he read so much.

"The Three Seasons?" Aunt Nan objected. "Who ever heard of three seasons? We can't have a club without you, Jake."

Jake patted her hand. "You can be the fourth season, Aunt Nan. Spring, fall, winter, summer. You can be whichever one you want."

"No," Aunt Nan said, "I'm just the adviser. You're the president."

They'd made him president because all along he'd protested. They thought by making him president they'd get him to stay, and it had worked for a while. But not forever, obviously. "It's because he's the only boy," Jenny explained. "He doesn't like the club because the rest of us are girls. Even Aunt Nan."

Aunt Nan turned to Jake. "Is that true?" she asked him.

"Yeah. I'd have quit a long time ago if you weren't such a good cook."

68

"Do you think you could stay until the Hanukkah party?" Aunt Nan asked.

"Even with four we're not enough for a play about the Maccabees," Sally said. "With three we couldn't do it at all. Please stay, Jake."

"You can't go home now anyway," Emily pointed out. "We won't be picked up until nine o'clock. No one's going to make a special trip just to get you."

"I can walk."

"Five miles?" Jenny said. "In the dark? Don't be silly."

Jake stood up. "I'm going into the bathroom," he said. "I'll sit on the toilet and read until it's time to go home."

"Please, Jake," Sally begged. "Don't ruin our show."

Emily jumped up too. "Jake, I have an idea. If we had another boy, would it be all right? Would you be in the play?"

"What are you talking about?" Jenny asked. "Where are we going to get another boy?"

"We could sure use one," Emily said. No one disagreed. They were all playing so many parts, they couldn't get into and out of their various bathrobes fast enough.

"But who?" Jenny asked. "Who would be willing to be in our family play?"

"Oh, cripes," Sally said, hitting her forehead with her hand. "I know who she's thinking of. She's thinking of that creep, Simeon."

"Yes," Emily said. "I am." Though Simeon wasn't sure he wanted to come, Emily had called Grandma earlier to pave the way, just in case he did accept the invitation.

"It's all right with me," Aunt Nan said.

"He's a creep," Sally reiterated.

"He didn't knock over the Christmas tree," Emily said.

"I know he didn't," Sally said. "But he's still a creep."

"He's a boy." Emily's voice underlined the last word.

"I'll check him out," Jake said.

"You mean it's all right with you?" Emily asked.

"I'll let you know tomorrow."

Turning first to Sally and then to Jenny,

Emily grinned triumphantly. She didn't say anything. She didn't have to.

Aunt Nan never let them clear the table. She didn't trust them to carry her Limoges into the kitchen. They left the dishes and moved over to the sofa and chairs. It was time to rehearse the play.

The Four Seasons always put on plays for family parties. The club had started one day at the beach when the Big Kids had gone for a bike ride and picnic to the lighthouse and told the Little Kids they couldn't come along. Aunt Nan had suggested a secret club as revenge. They held their first meeting late that afternoon on the beach. The Big Kids hung around, trying to hear what they were saying, so they moved down to the edge of the surf. The Big Kids said the club would last for two, maybe three meetings and then collapse. They said that was what happened to all little-kid clubs. Thanks to Aunt Nan, it did not happen to the Four Seasons. The club was into its second year. They'd realized early on that they needed something to do at their meetings besides eat Aunt Nan's super suppers. That's when

Sally came up with the idea of putting on a play in honor of Grandma's sixty-fifth birthday.

They surprised the whole family with that first production. It was called *The Great Happening,* and depicted Grandma's birth. Jenny, playing Great-Grandma, lay moaning on the sofa. Sally was Great-Grandpa. He brought the flaky doctor, played by Jake, a bowl of hot water, which the doctor proceeded to drink. Jake ad libbed that part. Emily was Grandma. She was born from under the blanket covering the couch. Aunt Nan wanted her to appear only in her underpants, but she insisted on wearing her pink-and-white quilted bathrobe. Since then they'd done a play for every family gathering, most often costumed in bathrobes of one sort or another. The fact that a play was going to be put on was no longer a surprise, but no matter how much Lisa, Chip, or Amy begged, no member of the Four Seasons let slip in advance the slightest hint of what the new play was about.

This was their second Hanukkah production. Last year they'd made a play out of a funny Hanukkah story by Isaac Bashevis Singer called "The First Schlemiel." But this year they had decided to be more serious. They were going to enact the real story of the first Hanukkah, the story of the Maccabees.

Using the ideas they'd talked about at their previous meeting, Aunt Nan had typed up a script and made copies of it on the copying machine at her office. Now she passed them out. "Jake can be Judah Maccabee," Sally said.

"No," Jake said. "I want to be the Syrian general. You can be Judah Maccabee."

"You know what, Jake? I'm going to make an idol," Jenny said. "A great big idol out of cardboard. You know, for you to make the Jews bow down to."

Jake leafed through the script. "Are there battles in here?" he asked.

"Of course," Aunt Nan said. "You get killed by Judah Maccabee."

"First I put up a good fight, and then I die." Jake leaped to his feet, put his hand to his throat, cried "Aargh," fell to the ground, writhed around for a couple of seconds, and then lay still, with his eyes shut. The others applauded. Jake leaped to his feet and bowed. "I'm the best at dying," he said. "That's why I have to be the Syrian general."

"Mattathias could die too," Sally suggested. "The general could kill him when he won't bow down to the false gods."

"But that's not how it happened," Jake said. "So we can't do it that way. We can't change history."

"The person who plays Mattathias has to change his costume and play other parts too," Aunt Nan explained. "He gets to be one of the other Maccabee brothers."

"I'll be Mattathias," Emily said. "I'm a quick dresser."

"All right," Aunt Nan said. "And then you can turn into Eleazar. Jenny, you can be John. I'm going to change the script a little. I'm going to put Simon Maccabee in the first scene and the last scene. That's the part your friend Simeon can play. They have almost the same name. In the middle he can be a Syrian. If we have two Syrians, instead of just one, the battles will look a little better."

Emily nodded. If Simeon didn't come, and they had to go back to having only one Syrian, it wouldn't matter too much.

"After he's killed, let Jake change his bathrobe too," Sally said. "He can be the fifth brother, Jonathan. That way we'll have all five Maccabee brothers in the last scene, where they restore the Temple."

They read through Aunt Nan's script. Jake added some jokes, though not as many as he wanted. Jenny wouldn't let him use the ones that were really corny. Jake and Sally fought a furious battle, using a broomstick and a mop handle for swords. Jenny said she'd make better swords, out of aluminum foil and cardboard, for all of them. Aunt Nan laid some old shirts on a chair so they could practice changing between scenes. Timing was important, she said. They didn't want the play to drag. "We can fit in only two more meetings before the party," she warned them. "Make sure you learn your parts." She turned to Emily. "Let me know as soon as you can if Simeon is coming. If he is, I can revise the script and get copies to all of you fast."

"I think I'll make that idol out of papier-mâché instead of cardboard," Jenny said. "Then we can knock it down and tear it up when we clean up the Temple. Mom will help me."

"Excellent!" Aunt Nan exclaimed. "A boffo ending."

"This is going to be our best play ever," Sally said.

"I could still decide not to be in it," Jake announced.

"You'll be in it," Emily said. "I know you'll be in it."

The next morning, on the bus, Petey and Gloria talked to each other. They didn't say a word to the twins. Then, before school began, Emily took some pencils out of her desk. One of them dropped from her hand and rolled down the aisle. Melody bent over to pick it up. "Don't touch it," Petey exclaimed. "It's full of cooties."

Melody sat up again and looked at Petey, puzzled.

"You'll get cooties if you touch that pencil," Petey said. "That's the Cootie Girl's pencil."

Melody turned a bright red. "Who's a Cootie Girl?" she asked. She sounded as if she were choking.

"Emily. Emily's a Cootie Girl. Didn't you know that?"

Emily rose and picked up her own pencil. She glared at Petey as she passed her. Petey lifted her desk top, pretending to look for something inside. Emily sat back down, took out a book, opened it up, and stared at the page in front of her, though she couldn't read a word. Petey had called her Cootie Girl. Maybe the others wouldn't actually use that terrible name for her too, but they'd stay away from her. Once you were branded "Cootie Girl," you could forget about friends. Melody, new in the third grade, had been Cootie Girl for six months. This year there hadn't been a Cootie Girl. Not until today.

Emily blinked her eyes hard several times to make sure she didn't cry. A Cootie Girl who cried didn't have a chance. She breathed deeply and tried to think about the Four Seasons meeting of the night before. Jenny. Jake. Aunt Nan. Fried chicken. The Maccabees. Anything to erase the cry of "Cootie Girl" from her mind.

At lunch Emily avoided the back section of the all-purpose room. She found a seat in the front, with some third graders. After a while Sally came and stood at the end of the table, her lunch bag in one hand and her carton of chocolate milk in the other. "What are you doing here?" she asked.

"I'm not sitting with Petey. She wouldn't let me sit with her anyway. She called me Cootie Girl this morning."

"Boy oh boy!" Sally said with a sigh. She pulled out the chair next to Emily and sat down. "You are causing me so much trouble. I can't stand it."

"Go ahead," Emily said. "Go ahead, sit with Petey and Gloria. I don't care."

"You know if I did you'd kill me." Sally unwrapped her sandwich and began eating.

"But we have to find a way out of this. We've been friends with Petey and Gloria too long to just forget about them."

"Petey called me Cootie Girl."

"Well," Sally replied calmly, "I didn't say it was going to be easy."

In the afternoon the whole school met in the all-purpose room to practice the Winter Concert. Five minutes after Simeon and Emily had settled themselves in the library, Jake showed up. He was grinning. He sat down at the table with them. "Simeon, this is my cousin Jake," Emily said.

"Hi, Jake," said Simeon.

"Hi, Simeon," said Jake. "I'm not singing Christmas carols either. I don't like to sing. But I told them it's because I'm Jewish."

Emily looked at Simeon and Simeon looked at Emily. She smiled a little; he raised his eyebrows and shrugged.

"You know what they're saying in the third grade?" Jake said. "They're saying you knocked over the Christmas tree."

"They're saying it in the fourth grade too," Simeon replied. "But I didn't."

"That's what Emily says. You didn't."

Once again, Simeon and Emily exchanged glances.

"I wish we knew how it really did fall over," Emily said with a sigh. "If we knew that, it would solve a lot of problems."

Simeon nodded. "We ought to find out."

"How could we do that?" Emily wanted to know.

"We could investigate," Simeon said.

"Yeah," Jake chimed in enthusiastically. "Like detectives. Like Encyclopedia Brown. I love Encyclopedia Brown books."

"So do I," Simeon admitted.

Emily's forehead wrinkled in a frown. She was thinking. "The first thing we have to do," she said slowly, "is talk to Mr. Oliver. He might know, from the way the tree was lying, whether it was knocked over, or whether it just fell down."

"If he says it just fell down, maybe we could get him to announce that over the intercom," Simeon suggested. "Tell him he has to do that to quiet down the rumors."

"And if he thinks it was knocked down, maybe he has some ideas about who did it,"

Jake added, his voice rising with excitement. "Maybe he heard or saw something that morning."

"But do you think he'll talk to us?" Simeon wondered. "We're not really detectives. We're only kids."

"Mr. Oliver is very nice," Emily assured him. "I think he'll talk to us. If we explain the problem, I think he'll want to help."

"Let's see if we can find him now," Jake suggested, "while we have the time." He glanced up at the clock on the library wall. "I think we have the time." Jake, the best reader in the third grade, was not so good with hours and minutes.

"We do," Simeon said. "They'll be rehearsing for another half hour."

Jake jumped up. "This is fun. I've never been a detective before." He started for the door and then, suddenly, he paused and turned. "Hey, Simeon, you coming to our party?"

"Your Hanukkah party?"

"Yeah. Emily was supposed to ask you."

"She asked me, quite a while ago."

Jake glanced at Emily, who smiled a little

and shrugged. "Well, are you coming?" Jake repeated, turning again to Simeon. "We need you. To be in our play. We need five Maccabee brothers. Right now we only have four." Emily noticed he didn't mention that Simeon would have to be a Syrian too.

Simeon pushed back the thick, sandy-colored shock of hair that was always falling down into his eyes. Emily figured he had to do that in order to see better. And he did pause for a moment and stare at Jake. Then he smiled. "Okay," he said. "I'll come."

Five

The lavatories, the large, brightly painted kindergarten, the all-purpose room, the storerooms, and the boiler room were in the basement of Watch Mountain School. So was Mr. Oliver's office. Emily knocked on the door. "Who's there?" Mr. Oliver called out.

"Emily Berg."

"Well, come on in."

Emily pushed open the door. Mr. Oliver's

office looked nothing like Mrs. Titus's. It contained no file cabinets and no desk—at least no desk that was usable, though two broken student desks stood in a corner, waiting for Mr. Oliver to get to them. One wall was covered with a pegboard, from which hung a hundred different kinds of tools. Against the opposite wall an old sofa rested, its springs sagging. A little table bearing an electric coffee pot and two chipped mugs leaned against it. In another corner a couple of barrels of cleaning compound and some brooms still in brown wrapping paper stood waiting to be put away in the storeroom that opened off the office. Old cabinets lined the walls. The door of one was open. Inside Emily could see coffee cans full of nails and screws, tubes of paste, paint cans and brushes. Mr. Oliver was sitting on a long bench at the table in the middle of the room. The floor-waxing machine was stretched out on the table, its motor exposed.

"That machine looks very sick," Jake said.

Mr. Oliver looked up. "Nothing too serious, I hope. If it is, I'll have to call in a specialist." His eyes moved from Jake to Emily to Simeon. "Who do we have here? Jake and Emily and . . . I don't think I know you."

"I'm Simeon. I'm new."

"How come you're not at the rehearsal?"

Across the hall in the all-purpose room, the whole school was singing "O Come, All Ye Faithful." Emily could hear the *thump-thump-thump* of Mr. Starrett's piano beneath the voices. "We're Jewish," she said. "We don't sing Christmas carols."

"Oh. That's interesting. Some Jews do."

"Everyone has to do what he or she thinks is right," Emily said.

Mr. Oliver nodded. "Okay, I'll buy that. So long as it doesn't hurt anyone else."

"If I don't sing in the Winter Concert, that doesn't hurt anyone," Simeon said. "But if someone says I knocked down the Christmas tree when I didn't, that hurts me!"

Mr. Oliver stood up. "Is that what they're saying?"

Simeon nodded.

"And you didn't?"

"Of course not."

"That's why we came here, Mr. Oliver. We thought maybe you could tell us whether that tree was knocked down, or whether it fell down," Emily said.

Mr. Oliver pointed to the sofa. "Make yourselves comfortable, kids." He sat too, on the end of his bench, facing them. "I'll be up-front with you guys," he said. "I think that tree was knocked down. I'm not saying you did it, Simeon. I have no reason to suspect you, no reason to suspect anyone in particular. But I think it was knocked down."

Simeon pushed back his hair. Emily frowned. So much for the hope that Mr. Oliver would make an announcement assuring the school that the tree had fallen accidentally. "Why do you think the tree was knocked down?" Jake asked.

"When I put it up in the first place, I really secured it," Mr. Oliver said. "After all, there's a lot of traffic in that corridor. You kids come in and out of the building like a herd of elephants. I had to make sure the vibrations from a hundred and fifty pairs of

clomping feet wouldn't make the tree fall over. Now, the stand is a real sturdy one, with a giant water reservoir. It was the biggest one I could find, for a very big tree. Yesterday someone said something about an earthquake. I tell you, that's what it would have taken to knock that tree over accidentally. An earthquake."

"Mr. Oliver," Emily asked, "what time did you come in yesterday?"

"Seven o'clock, same as always. I hung out the flag, and then I came down here to my office. I put up my coffee and got right to work repairing a desk." He gestured toward the corner. "Like those over there."

"Did you see or hear anything unusual?" Emily's dad liked to watch police shows on TV. Often, she watched with him. She knew what questions a detective should ask.

"I didn't think there was anyone else in the building. I thought I was alone. But of course someone could have come in the front door, and I wouldn't have known. This old building creaks when the herd of elephants is tromping through the upstairs hall, but you can't hear the noise just a couple of kids make, when you're down here." His eyes were wide and thoughtful; he was trying hard to remember. "I did hear the tree go over. I heard a big thump. I didn't know then what it was. I ran upstairs to find out. There was the tree, on the floor. I didn't see any sign of a human being. But what a mess there was in the hall! The biggest mess I've had to clean up since I came to this school, and I tell you, I've had to clean up some outstanding messes. But this was the champion. All that paper turned to mush by the spilled water. All that popcorn. Next year maybe we can get the first grade to do something besides popcorn."

"Next year," Jake said, "the tree won't be knocked over."

"I certainly hope not," Mr. Oliver said. "Only you know how these things are once they get started. What's to stop the same people who did it this year from doing it again next year? Or again this year, for that matter?"

"You said 'people,' " Simeon noted. "Do you think more than one person did it?"

Mr. Oliver nodded. "It's a big tree, and

this is a school full of little kids. It was more than one kid, or else it was the biggest sixth grader we've got."

"That'd be Hugo Rafferty," Emily said. "I don't think Hugo would knock over a Christmas tree."

"Neither do I," said Mr. Oliver. "Even though he's almost as tall as I am, and twice as broad, he's gentle as a rabbit."

"Have you and Mrs. Titus talked this over?" Simeon wanted to know.

"Yes," Mr. Oliver said. "I told her that tree could never have fallen by itself. She agrees, but she doesn't know what we can do about it. We don't have a clue."

"Mrs. Titus could cross-examine every student in the school," Jake suggested. "She could bring them into her office one by one and ask them questions. I bet the guilty one would squirm a lot. Then she'd know."

"Come on, Jake," Mr. Oliver said. "Do you have any idea how long it would take to interview every one of the hundred and fifty kids in this school?"

"Well, the teachers could help," Jake said. "They could cross-examine their students first, and then send the ones who squirmed a lot to Mrs. Titus."

"You know, I think that may be against the law," Mr. Oliver said. "I think maybe you can't ask people a lot of questions unless you have some reason to be suspicious of them."

"The guilty person might not squirm at all," Emily said. "And some innocent people might squirm a lot. They might just be uncomfortable answering a lot of questions and squirm. I know I would."

"I would too," Simeon said glumly. "Just knowing some people *thought* I'd done it would be enough to make me squirm."

"It's impossible," Emily agreed. "You can't question every kid in the school. You have to find a clue. Somewhere, there has to be a clue."

Simeon's shoulders slumped. "If Mr. Oliver was the only person in the building, and he didn't see or hear anyone, what kind of clue are we going to find?"

"Hey, Simeon, don't give up!" Jake exclaimed. "We'll work on it. I'll keep reading Encyclopedia Brown. Maybe I'll get an idea.

But I think the most important thing is for us to keep our eyes and our ears open. You never know what we might see or hear. That means you too, Simeon. Three pairs of eyes and ears are better than two."

"Well, I'll keep mine open too," said Mr. Oliver. "Four pairs are better than three. If I find anything out, I'll let you know."

Simeon glanced at his watch. "We'd better get back to our classrooms. The rehearsal across the hall will be over any minute now. If our teachers see us, they'll get mad. This isn't where we're supposed to be."

Mr. Oliver grinned. "My lips are sealed."

After school Emily called Aunt Nan at work. "Simeon's coming to the party. Jake said it's okay."

"I'll get revised scripts to you tomorrow," Aunt Nan returned. "You can give one to him. Tell him to come to the rehearsal Thursday night."

"I guess we'll have to pick him up," Emily said. "I'd better get Mom to call his mother."

"You're so efficient, darling," said Aunt

Nan. "When you grow up you'll be a business tycoon, not just a plain old secretary, like me."

"Thanks, Aunt Nan. I'll see you tomorrow. Good-bye."

"Good-bye, darling."

Emily hung up with a sigh. To Aunt Nan she wasn't any Cootie Girl. There was some comfort in that. Not a lot, but some.

Next, Emily called Grandma. She told her Simeon was definitely coming to the party. "That's super," Grandma said, as Emily had known she would. "Any friend of yours is a friend of mine."

Emily made a third phone call. She dialed Simeon and told him about the rehearsal. "I'll come," Simeon said, "if it's okay with my folks."

"Listen, Simeon. About the other thing— the tree—I had an idea."

"What?"

"You walk to school," Emily said. "You don't have to wait for the bus. You can go anytime. So why don't you go real early for a few days in a row? Hang around, see if anyone else shows up early."

"Not a bad idea." Simeon sounded excited—for Simeon. "As far as we know now, any one of a hundred and fifty kids might have knocked over that tree."

"Or any two, or any three," Emily remarked.

"Right. But if I find out who hangs around the school early in the morning, at least we'll have a place to start. I'll be there by seven on Monday."

"I hope it's not too cold." Emily pictured Simeon's ears and fingers turning blue and his legs aching as he climbed up and down the front steps of the school building for an hour in an effort to keep warm.

"Doesn't matter," Simeon said. "I can take it."

They said good-bye and hung up. Emily turned and saw Sally standing in the doorway, gazing at her with a question in her eyes. "Why do you want Simeon to go to school early?" she asked.

"It's a secret," Emily said. "Only me and Simeon and Jake and Mr. Oliver know."

"You can tell me," Sally said. "I promise I won't tell."

Emily lowered her voice to a whisper. "We've started an investigation. We're going to find out who really knocked over the tree."

"Why is that a secret?"

"If the one who did it finds out we're after him, he'll get real careful. But if he thinks no one suspects, he may get careless. He may do or say something that'll be a clue."

"Oh."

Emily returned to her normal tone of voice. "Well, as long as you know, if you hear or see something, let us know. Five pairs of eyes and ears are better than four." She wasn't sure that was true. There might come a point at which more pairs of eyes and ears would be just too many. She wasn't going to tell anyone else about the investigation. Knowing Jake, she suspected he'd already told Jenny. But that was where it would stop. She'd warn Jake not to tell anyone else. She didn't have to worry about Simeon. He didn't have anyone to tell.

Tuesday morning, before class began,

Simeon, Emily, and Jake stood outside the door to the fourth-grade room, talking in low voices. It was the second day Simeon had watched for early arrivals. The day before he'd seen no one, except Mr. Oliver and some teachers. "But you know who showed up today?" he said. "You'll never guess."

"Frankenstein," said Jake. "Rambo. Oscar the Grouch."

"Shut up, Jake," Emily exclaimed impatiently. She turned to Simeon. "The bell's going to ring soon. There's no time to guess. Just tell us."

"Gloria."

"Gloria!" Emily repeated. But then she realized that was really no surprise. "Of course. Lots of mornings she's not on the bus. Her mother hates to get up early, so her father takes her to the diner for breakfast and then drops her at school on his way to work. But I never thought about Gloria. What reason would she have to knock over the tree?"

"I didn't say she knocked over the tree,"

Simeon returned sharply. "I just said she came to school early."

Emily sighed. "So that's a clue that's not a clue. Boy, being a detective is tough."

"Just because you don't think Gloria did it doesn't mean she didn't do it," Jake warned.

"Yeah," Simeon agreed. "You have to talk to her, Emily."

"Me?"

"You're her friend."

"Not anymore I'm not. Petey and Gloria call me Cootie Girl."

"Gloria never has, has she? It's Petey who's done that."

"Well, if Petey does it, Gloria agrees with it."

"Try talking to her at home," Simeon suggested. "If Petey's not around, she may act different."

Walk up Gloria's driveway? Ring Gloria's doorbell? It was impossible. Emily shook her head.

"You have to," Simeon said. "You just have to."

Emily's eyes were fixed on her sneakers. "No I don't."

"Take Sally with you," Jake said.

She lifted her chin and looked at him, her eyes widening. Maybe that would work. No one had called Sally Cootie Girl. "I'll think about it," she said.

Neither Emily nor Sally could have gone to Gloria's house that afternoon, because they had Hebrew school over in New Hebron. Emily talked to Sally about visiting Gloria the next day. She said she'd come.

Wednesday morning Simeon had more news. "Gloria didn't come to school early today," he told Emily and Jake.

"I know," Emily said. "She was on the bus."

"But two other people did!" He paused dramatically. "Guess who."

"Go-Bot," said Jake. "Superman. Bill Cosby."

"Rusty Milletta," Simeon announced, "and Adam Finkel." He touched the crocheted cap on the back of his head. "They knocked off my kipah again," he continued. "The way they always do whenever they see me. And then they went into the building. It was unlocked. Mr. Oliver and Mrs. Titus were already here."

"You followed them," Jake whispered.

"Yes. Not too close. I didn't want them to know I was following them. I was scared. They're so big."

"Not as big as Hugo Rafferty," said Jake.

"Big enough. If they turned around and saw me, they'd do a lot more than knock off my kipah."

"I think you were very brave," Emily assured him. "Kids aren't even supposed to be in the building before ten of eight. If Mrs. Titus had seen you, she'd have gotten real mad."

Simeon nodded, his face serious. "Yes. But I figured if Rusty and Adam weren't worried about Mrs. Titus, I wasn't going to worry about her either."

"Well," Jake urged, "where did Rusty and Adam go?"

Simeon sighed. "Only into the boys' room."

"What happened in there?"

"I don't know. I didn't follow them in."

"You missed your big chance!" Jake exclaimed.

"Would you have done it?" Simeon asked. "Would you have gone into the lav, just you and two huge, mean sixth graders, when it was too early for anyone else to come in and stop them from doing whatever they felt like doing to you?"

"I guess not," Jake admitted.

"Sally and I are walking over to Gloria's after school today," Emily said. "I'll let you know what I find out."

Jake rubbed his hands together. "This is getting good," he said. "I wish I could come too." But of course he couldn't. He wasn't Gloria's friend, and he lived too far from her anyway.

Even for the twins it was a twenty-minute walk. After school they ate bread spread with peanut butter and jelly, drank a glass of milk, and set out.

"This could be a big hike for nothing," Emily said. "I hope today isn't Brownies or something." Emily and Sally didn't belong to Brownies. Their mother thought Hebrew School and music lessons were enough.

Anyway, they had the Four Seasons. "Or suppose Petey's there," Emily added. "Then what do we do?" She was already sorry she'd let Simeon and Jake talk her into this whole trip.

"Petey won't be there," Sally said. "Gloria usually goes to Petey's house. Petey almost never goes to Gloria's."

"Well, then, that's where she could be. Let's go back."

"She isn't," Sally said. "She's home."

"How do you know?"

"I spoke to her in school today."

"You told her we were coming?"

Sally nodded.

"And she said okay?"

"She said that would be fine."

Emily's eyes widened in amazement. "She doesn't mind the Cootie Girl in her house?"

"Gloria goes along with Petey," Sally said thoughtfully, "but I'm beginning to think she doesn't always agree with her."

Emily walked a little faster. Maybe Simeon was right. Separate Gloria from Petey and maybe she'd develop some opinions of her own.

They rang Gloria's back doorbell. Gloria's mother opened the door. She was wearing a robe and slippers and holding a chocolate-chip cookie in her hand. "Hi, twinsies," she said. She worked at night and had probably just gotten out of bed. "Want some?"

"No thanks," Sally said. "We just ate."

Mrs. Blake sat down at the table and sipped her coffee. Gloria was sitting at the table too, a plate of cookies and a glass of Coke in front of her. They were both watching a soap opera on TV. Emily had been to Gloria's house before. She knew there was a TV set in the living room, one in the family room, and one in each of the bedrooms. That meant the only rooms without TVs were the bathrooms. Gloria was lucky. The Bergs' house was a lot bigger than the Blakes', and in the whole place there were only two TVs. There'd be three if Sally got what she wanted for Hanukkah.

"We'll go into my room," Gloria said. "Mom, remember what happens so you can tell me later."

"Nothing will happen," Mrs. Blake said. But she didn't take her eyes off the set.

"Tell me anyway," Gloria said. She picked up the plate of cookies and the glass of Coke and led the way into her room. "You want to play rock stars?" she asked. "I have Michael Jackson paper dolls and Prince paper dolls and Madonna paper dolls—a set for each of us. I choose Madonna."

They each set their dolls and their clothes up in a separate corner of the room. The bed was the sports arena or the park or the recording studio where they all came together to perform. They tuned in to the MTV channel and pretended their dolls were singing the songs. Sally sang along right from the beginning. Soon Emily and Gloria joined in too.

"This is fun," Emily said. "Thanks for letting me come, even though I'm a Cootie Girl."

Gloria fastened the tabs of a black miniskirt around Madonna's waist. "I don't think you're a Cootie Girl," she said softly. "Petey thinks you are, but I don't."

"Petey thinks I'm a Cootie Girl because I won't sing Christmas carols and because

Simeon's my friend," Emily said. "She thinks Simeon knocked down the Christmas tree. Do you think so?"

Gloria didn't look up. Emily couldn't see her face, only the sweep of her thick, straight, shoulder-length black hair. She didn't say anything.

"Well, do you?" Emily asked again. "Do you think Simeon knocked over the Christmas tree?"

Gloria mumbled something.

Emily couldn't understand her. "What did you say?"

Her cheeks had turned as red as the turtleneck she was wearing. "I don't know anything about the Christmas tree. I don't know who knocked it over, and I don't care!" she exclaimed vehemently.

Sally and Emily exchanged glances. Sally spoke in a gentle voice. "We just thought . . . well, since you get to school so early sometimes, you might have seen something that day. The day the tree fell. We'd like to find out who really did knock it down, so people won't blame Simeon anymore."

"I'm sorry they're blaming Simeon,"

Gloria said. "I really am. But I don't know who did it. I don't have any idea. How would I know something like that?" She swept all the Madonna paper doll clothes together into a pile and then began to put them away in a shoe box. "Look, it's getting late. You guys better go now. I have to help my mom get supper."

"But she just finished breakfast," Emily said.

"Our supper, her lunch." Sally started to return the Michael Jackson paper dolls to their shoe box. "Don't bother to put them away," Gloria said. "I can do that later, after my mom goes to work. You just go on home now."

Emily and Sally put on their coats. Gloria walked with them to the kitchen. Mrs. Blake wasn't there any longer, though the TV was still playing. Gloria opened the back door. "Good-bye," she said.

"Good-bye," the twins murmured. They stepped outside. Gloria slammed the door behind them.

"Boy!" Emily exclaimed. "I never saw anything like that. We were having such a good time, and then she got rid of us so fast you'd think we both really had cooties."

Sally nodded, her face serious. "Something's going on," she said. "Something's going on for sure."

"Yeah," Emily agreed. "She knows something about the Christmas tree. I know she does. But you can bet we won't be in her house again anytime soon. How are we ever going to get her to tell us what she knows?"

Six

Mr. Oliver rolled the cart containing the TV and the VCR into the fourth-grade room a little before two in the afternoon. Melody jumped up and then plopped down again. "What are we going to see? What are we going to see?" she exclaimed.

"It's a special treat," Mrs. Glendenning said. She often had a special treat for them the last few minutes of school, but this was an hour and a half before the final bell would ring. "A *special* special treat," she amended.

Mr. Oliver placed the cart at the front of the room and plugged in the machines. "What's the show today?" he asked.

"Dickens' *A Christmas Carol*," Mrs. Glendenning said. "The TV version starring George C. Scott."

"Oh boy," said Mr. Oliver. "I wish I could stay and watch."

"Why don't you?" Emily invited.

"I have too much work to do." He turned and moved toward the door.

"You ought to take Simeon and Emily with you," Petey called out.

Mr. Oliver stopped and turned back again. "What's that?"

"People who don't sing Christmas carols won't want to watch Christmas movies," Petey said. "Especially one called *A Christmas Carol*."

Watching a movie or reading a story wasn't the same thing as singing the words of Christmas songs yourself. Couldn't Petey understand that? "I do too want to watch it," Emily shouted.

Petey paid no more attention to Emily than she would have to a fly. She stared at Simeon. "People who knock over Christmas trees don't deserve to watch Christmas movies." She spoke slowly, pronouncing each word carefully.

"Petey!" Mrs. Glendenning's voice was sharp. "I told you before. Don't make accusations you can't prove."

Petey tossed her head. "I didn't name anyone," she said. "I think it's terrible that a person can do a bad thing in this school and get away with it. It's not fair. He should be punished." A murmur ran through the classroom. It sounded to Emily like a murmur of agreement.

Mrs. Glendenning stood in front of Petey's desk. "We don't know who knocked over the Christmas tree," she said. "We don't know. If I hear you making accusations again, you'll be the one who won't be seeing any Christmas movies."

Petey pressed her lips together, folded her hands on her desk, and stared straight ahead. Mrs. Glendenning turned to say good-bye to Mr. Oliver. Then she put the videotape in the machine. "It's not fair," Petey mouthed. She didn't have to say it out loud. Everyone understood her.

Later, on the bus ride home, Sally treated Emily to a critical analysis of the film. "I thought it was pretty good," she said. "If it ever turns up on TV again, I'll watch it. But I wouldn't ask Mom to go to the trouble of renting it for the VCR."

Emily wasn't paying much attention to Sally's conversation. She was looking at Petey and Gloria. Petey hadn't spoken to either of the twins, and neither had Gloria, because she was with Petey. But Gloria wasn't looking at Petey. She was staring straight ahead. Her face wore a worried frown. She looked as if she were thinking of something a lot more troublesome than Petey's chatter. Every once in a while her eyes would wander in Emily's direction. Then she'd blush and look away again.

That night at the Four Seasons meeting Emily told Simeon about Gloria's strange behavior. "Sally and I have to talk to her again," she said. "We've got to get her alone and talk to her. We couldn't this afternoon. She got off the bus at Petey's house."

"She was at school early today," Simeon said. "Not yesterday. But Rusty and Adam were there yesterday *and* today. Let's see. . . ." He counted the days off on his fingers. "I've come to school early four mornings. Gloria's come early on two of them, and so have Rusty and Adam, once when Gloria was there too."

"What do they do?" Emily asked.

"If it's nice out, Gloria plays on the swings. If it isn't nice, she waits in the vestibule. If Mr. Oliver and Mrs. Titus aren't around, Rusty and Adam go down into the boys' room. Otherwise they hang out in the playground too. First, of course, they knock off my kipah." He patted his crocheted cap as if to make sure it was still there.

"I guess you don't have to go anymore," Jake said. "I guess you've found out all you're going to find out."

"I'll come early a few more days," Simeon said, "just to make sure they're the only ones."

"Did Rusty and Adam tease Gloria this morning?" Emily asked. "Like they tease you?"

"No," Simeon responded. "And I think that's funny. Why do they bother me and leave her alone? Is it because she's a girl?"

Emily shook her head. "In the fall, when we were still having recess on the playground, if we were outside the same time as the sixth grade, and no teacher was looking, they bothered every kid they could get hold of. Boy or girl, they didn't care."

Sally nodded her agreement. "They pulled my ponytail so hard a couple of times, I just decided to let my hair go loose."

"Sometimes they tease the fifth-grade girls too," Jenny said. "They leave the fifth-grade boys alone. They're already getting too big for Adam and Rusty to fool with."

"Yeah," Simeon said. "They're only interested in you if you're small. That's what I don't understand. Gloria is *very* small."

Sally nodded. "She's the smallest kid in the class, and she probably eats the most."

Aunt Nan looked at Simeon's plate.

"Hard-boiled eggs and cottage cheese isn't much of a dinner," she said. The others had consumed huge portions of spaghetti and meat balls. Simeon was kosher; he could eat only foods prepared according to Jewish dietary laws. Aunt Nan didn't keep kosher. She had to feed Simeon on a paper plate and give him foods untouched by her cooking utensils.

"It's all right," Simeon said. "It was very good. I *like* cottage cheese."

"You're crazy," said Jake.

"Grandma keeps kosher," Emily assured Simeon. "You'll be able to eat at her house the day of the Hanukkah party."

After supper they rehearsed the play about the Maccabees. Simeon ad libbed some lines. "We'll keep them," Aunt Nan said. "They're good." In the big battle scene Simeon died almost as well as Jake.

When Emily's mother came to pick them up, Simeon went into the bedroom with Emily and the others to get his coat. Aunt Nan kissed the twins, Jenny, and Jake good night. Simeon, his hands at his sides, stood looking up at her. "Thank you very much," he said. "I had a very good time. I think the play is good. You're a good writer, and I bet you're a good cook too."

"Thank *you*, Simeon. I'm glad you could come." Aunt Nan put her hand on his shoulder. "Would it be all right if I kissed you good night too?"

"It would be all right," said Simeon in a low voice.

Aunt Nan kissed the top of his head. "Good night, Simeon," she said.

Lying in bed that night, the lights out, Emily and Sally made plans. "If only we could get to school early, like Simeon," Emily said. "That would be a good time to talk to Gloria. You know she isn't going to let us into her house again, and the rest of the day she's with Petey. She won't even talk to us when she's with Petey."

"Dad has tennis on Tuesday morning," Sally said. "We'll get him to drop us off first. Simeon said Gloria was there last Tuesday. She'll probably be there this coming Tuesday too. I think Tuesday is one of the days her father usually takes her out for breakfast. Tuesdays and Thursdays."

"You know," Emily said, "I just thought of something."

"What?"

"The tree was knocked down on a Thursday. Last Thursday. One week ago today."

"Yes," Sally said. "I know."

At breakfast, Emily talked to her father. "Listen, Dad," she said, "we want you to take us to school Tuesday on your way to tennis. Would that be all right?"

"That's awfully early," Mr. Berg said. "What do you want to be there at seven-thirty for?"

Emily looked at Sally and Sally looked at Emily. They had agreed not to tell anyone at home that they were playing detective. Simeon and Jake felt the same. It was not something the grown-ups could be expected to understand. "We're working on a mural," Emily said. This was true. "We don't get enough time for it during school." This was not true.

"Since we ride the bus," Sally added, "we

don't get any other time for it either. If we could come early once or twice, it would help."

"All right," their father agreed. "But you have to get up at six-fifteen. If you're not ready by the time I leave, I'm going without you. I can't be late for my game. It wouldn't be fair to the other guys."

They set their alarm clock half an hour ahead. When it rang, Emily thought it was still the middle of the night, and she stretched to switch it off before it woke the rest of the family. She glimpsed the day outside the window. It wasn't still night, but the sun would never rise that morning. It was a dreary, drizzly, gray day, the kind of day when the thing you want to do most is stay in bed.

Sally turned over with a groan. "Let's skip it," she muttered. "We can do it Thursday."

"Thursday may be too late," Emily said briskly. She hopped out of bed. "By Thursday Petey may have arranged to hang Simeon from the nearest tree. But I'll go myself if you don't want to come."

"I'm coming, I'm coming."

They were ready to go at seven-fifteen exactly. When their father dropped them off in front of the school building, Emily noticed that someone was already standing in the vestibule. It was too wet for the playground. Climbing the stairs, she realized it was Simeon, waiting. He was alone.

"Gloria didn't come?" Emily asked as she pulled open the door. "Phooey. I don't know how we'll get here another day."

Simeon glanced at his watch. "It's early. She doesn't show up until around twenty to eight."

"What about Rusty and Adam?" Sally asked. "Are they down in the boys' room?"

"No. They walk over. Too wet for them today, I guess. They must have decided to wait for the bus."

It was damp and chilly in the unheated vestibule. Emily hopped from one foot to the other in an effort to get her blood running. "It's no fun showing up here early," she said to Simeon. "Pretty neat of you to come so many days in a row."

"It's just my job. A detective does what he has to do." Emily couldn't tell whether he was serious or kidding. He wasn't smiling, but that didn't mean anything. Simeon hardly ever smiled.

A van pulled up to the curb. The door opened and Gloria stepped out. She slammed the door and came running up the walk. She climbed the steps and pushed open the door. "Twinsies!" she cried in surprise. "Why aren't you riding the bus?"

"We wanted to talk to you," Emily said.

Gloria backed herself into the corner between the front door and the side wall. "You can talk to me anytime," she said. "In class. On the bus. You didn't have to come early just for that."

"You're always with Petey," Sally explained. "You don't talk to us when Petey's around."

"This'll all be over after Christmas," Gloria said. She looked at Sally, then looked away again. "I'm sure it will be. After vacation the four of us will be friends again."

"I hope so," Sally said.

Emily saw no point in mentioning that she wasn't at all sure she wanted to be friends with Petey anymore. "You're here early a lot of mornings, aren't you, Gloria?" she asked.

Gloria glanced at Simeon. He was leaning quietly against the opposite wall, watching her steadily. "Yeah," she said at last. "My dad takes me to the diner sometimes. We have to go early, so he can make it to work on time. After breakfast he drops me here."

"Two Thursdays ago," Emily said. "Maybe he dropped you here early two Thursdays ago."

Gloria didn't reply. She turned and pressed her nose against one of the glass panes on the door as if she were expecting someone very important to appear.

"Do you remember what happened that Thursday?" Sally asked.

Gloria didn't turn around. But she shook her head.

"The Christmas tree got knocked over," Emily said. "How could you forget?"

Now Gloria turned. "I told you, I don't know anything about the Christmas tree. Nothing. Nothing at all." Her face was

white, and with her arms crossed over her chest, she hugged herself tightly. "What makes you think I do?"

Now Emily was sure she did. Absolutely sure.

Sally reached out and touched Gloria's folded arm. "Oh, please, Gloria, please," she said. "Tell us what happened that day. Please. Everyone thinks Simeon did it." Emily thought it was clever of Sally to say "everyone" instead of "Petey."

Sally's hand dropped to her side. "No one will talk to Simeon. Is that fair? And they made Emily Cootie Girl just because she's Simeon's friend. Is that fair? And they're even mean to me, just because I'm Emily's sister. Is that fair? Oh, Gloria, you know it isn't. Help us, please."

"I can't tell you," Gloria whispered. She looked like a rabbit facing the barrel of a hunter's gun. "I can't. If I tell you, they'll kill me."

"Who'll kill you?" Emily asked.

Simeon spoke up sharply. "Rusty and Adam. That's who."

"Is that right, Gloria?" Sally questioned. Gloria didn't move.

"They can't kill you," Emily said. "Not now. Don't you see? Everyone would know it was them."

"How?" Gloria's voice was barely a croak.

"We'd tell, of course," Emily said.

"Then they'd kill *you*." Gloria's voice sounded a little stronger.

"They can't kill everyone," Simeon responded. "If everyone knows they did it, they can't kill everyone." He stepped forward. "They did do it, didn't they? They knocked over the tree, you saw, and they made you promise not to tell."

Gloria stared at Simeon. And then, very slowly, she nodded. "It was raining," she said. "Like today. When I came into the vestibule, they were already here. I stood as far away from them as I could. But they weren't paying any attention to me. They were having an argument. It had something to do with a dirt bike. Rusty had borrowed Adam's dirt bike, and when he brought it back, it was all scratched up, like Rusty had been in an accident or something."

Once Gloria started to tell the story, it seemed as if she couldn't wait to get it all out. Her words tumbled forward, one on top of the other. "Adam wanted Rusty to pay for having it painted. But Rusty said he wouldn't. He said it was scratched when he got it. So Adam took a punch at Rusty. Rusty ducked and ran. He ran right through the door and into the hall. Adam ran after him. I didn't go in—I watched through the glass. Adam caught up with Rusty in front of the tree. He was hitting Rusty all over the place. Rusty hit him back, but he couldn't punch as hard as Adam. He was going to fall. To stop himself, he grabbed a branch of the tree. Adam grabbed Rusty. Rusty fell anyway, and he took the whole tree over with him." She giggled a little. "It was pretty funny. Because Adam fell too, and there they were, all mixed up with the tree, the popcorn, the water, everything."

Emily and Sally smiled too, picturing it. Even Simeon smiled.

"They got up," Gloria continued. "They tried to brush themselves off, but they were a mess. I could see them talking to each other, though I couldn't hear what they were saying. I guess they decided they had to go home and change or something, because they came back out. That's when they saw me." Suddenly she stopped talking. She wasn't giggling anymore.

"What happened?" Emily prompted.

"Adam grabbed one of my arms and Rusty grabbed the other. They squeezed real tight. They said if I told anyone they'd knocked over the tree, they'd knock me over, and they'd step on me and step on me until I looked like a pancake. That's what they said. I believed them. They'd do that. You know they would."

"But the morning I was here with all three of you, they left you alone," Simeon pointed out. "They knocked off my kipah, but they left you alone."

Gloria stared at him, her eyes wide.

"Don't you see?" Simeon pounded his fist into his hand. "They're just as afraid of you as you are of them!"

Gloria's mouth dropped open. It seemed to be the first time that thought had occurred to her.

"So if you tell what you saw," Emily explained, "they won't do anything to you. They wouldn't dare. Mrs. Titus won't let them. They'd be expelled if they did anything to you."

"So will you tell?" Sally asked. "Will you? All you have to do is go up to Mrs. Glendenning and whisper the story in her ear. She'll take it from there."

"I don't like to tattle," Gloria said.

"Of course not," Sally agreed soothingly, "but you have to when someone who's innocent is being accused of the crime!"

"Sally and I will go with you if you want us to," Emily said. "Won't we, Sally?"

Gloria shook her head. "No, I'll do it. I have to tell Petey first. Petey will really be mad at me if I don't."

Emily nodded. She could understand that.

Gloria glanced over at Simeon. "Look, Simeon," she said, "I'm sorry."

Simeon said nothing. Emily poked him in the side.

"I really am," Gloria said, taking a step in his direction. "But I was scared. I'm still scared," she added bluntly.

Simeon looked at Emily, and then he looked at Gloria. "It's all right," he said. "It's okay." He didn't sound happy about it, but at least he said it. Emily figured that under the circumstances, he'd gone about as far as he could go.

The door opened. It was Mrs. Glendenning, along with Mr. Starrett and the first-grade teacher, Miss Falcone. "Good morning, girls," she said when she saw them. "Good morning, Simeon. Oh, it's such a miserable morning. You kids don't have to wait here. Come on along to the room. I've got work for you to do."

"I'll wait for Petey, if that's okay," Gloria said. "The buses will be here soon."

The door opened again. Some other walkers were arriving. The twins and Simeon accompanied Mrs. Glendenning down the hall. When they got to the classroom, she told the twins to straighten out the supply closet and Simeon to neaten up the books and games in the reading corner. Emily, deep inside the closet arranging piles of construction paper by color, didn't even see Gloria and Petey arrive. But later, when the bell rang and she came out, she noticed them at Mrs. Glendenning's desk, talking quietly.

They kept talking right through morning announcements. Usually Mrs. Glendenning had to shout to get the fourth grade to shut up while Mrs. Titus spoke over the intercom. Today no one said a word. They were all straining to hear the intense conversation taking place in the front of the room. But no matter how they stretched their ears, they couldn't figure out what was going on. Emily, Sally, and Simeon knew, but they were as quiet as all the others. One thing everyone could tell: From the expressions on the three faces at Mrs. Glendenning's desk, the whole class could see the discussion was extremely serious.

Finally, Petey took her seat. Mrs. Glendenning scribbled a note and handed it to Gloria. Gloria left the room. Emily figured she was on her way to Mrs. Titus.

Mrs. Glendenning called the Gremlin reading group to the table in the back. Emily and Sally were both in that group. So were Simeon and Petey and four other kids. Back in September they'd argued for a week over a name for their group. It was Petey who'd come up with "Gremlin."

When they were all seated, Mrs. Glendenning looked at Petey. "Now?" Petey asked.

Mrs. Glendenning nodded.

Petey faced Simeon, sitting across the table. "I'm sorry, Simeon," she said in a low voice. "I'm sorry I said you knocked over the Christmas tree."

Simeon looked up from the book on the table in front of him and then looked down again. Slowly, he nodded.

"Who, then?" Melody exclaimed. "Who did knock it over?"

"It wouldn't be right for me to tell you," Mrs. Glendenning said. "Mrs. Titus has to speak to them first. Gloria could have been mistaken."

"She wasn't mistaken," Petey said. "She *saw*."

"Yes," said Mrs. Glendenning. "Seeing with your own eyes is different from jumping to conclusions without anything in the way of evidence."

Petey looked down at her book. The others weren't very interested in the story they were supposed to be reading. They wanted to talk about the Christmas tree. But Mrs. Glendenning wouldn't let them. She made them start the lesson.

Twenty minutes later Gloria returned to the room. She couldn't say much during math. But it was possible to talk during art. She whispered Adam's and Rusty's names to Melody, and Melody told Tommy, and Tommy told Robert. In five minutes the news was all over the class. At lunchtime Emily discovered it was all over the school. Adam and Rusty had been with Mrs. Titus for nearly an hour. Everyone in the sixth grade knew that, and everyone in the sixth grade knew why. When all the fourth graders knew, and all the sixth graders knew, it didn't take long for everyone else in the building to know too.

Emily and Sally stood in line to buy milk and ice-cream sandwiches. "Listen," Sally said, "today let's go back to our old table. Let's sit with Petey and Gloria."

"You can if you want to," Emily said.

"You know I won't unless you do too," Sally said.

"Petey says I'm a Cootie Girl," Emily reminded her.

"I don't think she'll say that anymore," Sally said.

"I'm not going to give her the chance," Emily said.

"She told Simeon she was sorry. In front of the whole reading group. That was hard. I think we have to make the next move," Sally said.

"Go ahead," Emily said. "Count me out."

"Please, Emily," Sally begged. "We've been friends with Petey and Gloria for a hundred years." She picked a carton of chocolate milk out of the refrigerated box and dropped it on Emily's tray. Then she grabbed a carton of plain milk for herself. "If I get a TV for our room for Hanukkah,

I'll let you pick the programs every night for two weeks."

"For a month," said Emily.

"For three weeks," said Sally.

Emily sighed and shrugged her shoulders. "Okay," she said. "I'll go over to the table with you. I'll sit with them, if they'll let me. But I won't say anything."

"You don't have to say anything, Emily. Not if you don't want to." Head high, Sally carried her tray across the all-purpose room and sat down with Petey and Gloria as if she'd never sat anywhere else. Emily followed, wondering what would happen.

"Hello, Sally," Petey said.

"Hello, Petey."

Emily was still standing. "Hello, Emily," Petey added.

Emily didn't speak. But she sat down.

They ate their lunch. Sally, Petey, and Gloria talked. Gloria had the most to say. She had so much to say that she hardly had time to finish her own sandwich, let alone Petey's. She told them what had happened when she went into Mrs. Titus' office. She seemed happy to be telling them. It was the first time in Emily's memory that Gloria had done the talking while Petey remained silent. They talked about Adam and Rusty too. "I wonder what's going to happen to them," Petey said.

"It was kind of an accident," Sally pointed out. "They didn't mean to knock over the tree."

"But they're not supposed to be inside the building before school," Petey said. "And they're certainly not supposed to be fighting."

"What makes it worse is that they kept quiet about it for so long," Gloria said.

"And they threatened you," Sally added. "That was really bad."

Petey nodded. "Oh, they'll get it. They'll get it, all right." Suddenly she turned and looked at Emily. She looked her right in the eye. "You're not a Cootie Girl," she said. "You never were a Cootie Girl." She raised her eyebrows. "But I still think Simeon is weird."

Emily took a deep breath. "I don't think so," she said. "Not anymore. But that's because I know him, and you don't. He's coming to our family Hanukkah party. He's going to be in our play."

"He's good," Sally said.

"What do you do at a Hanukkah party?" Petey wanted to know. She leaned forward, her elbow on the table, her chin resting on her hand.

"Well, we do a lot of things," Sally said. "We light the candles, and we open presents, and we sing songs, and we eat. Then we have the play. Each year it's about something different."

"Not every family has a play," Emily said. "Just our family, because we have the Four Seasons club with our aunt and our cousins, and that's what the club does. It puts on plays."

"That sounds neat," Petey said. "I don't have any cousins around here. They all live hundreds of miles away, and I hardly know them."

"Hey," Emily said, "you want to come?" She looked at Petey, and then she looked at Gloria. "You guys want to come to our

Hanukkah party Sunday afternoon?" She turned to Sally. "It'll be all right. I'm sure it'll be all right."

Sally looked into Emily's eyes, and then she laughed. "Emily, you're crazy," she said.

"We don't have to come," Petey said hastily.

"No, that's not what I mean," Sally said, holding up her hand. "I'm just laughing about something Emily said earlier. It's nothing. We both think it would be nice for you to come. I'm sure our grandmother won't mind."

"She'll be glad." Suddenly Emily felt like inviting the whole fourth grade, including Mrs. Glendenning. Especially including Mrs. Glendenning. But she couldn't do that. Even Grandma didn't have enough room for twenty-three extra guests.

"Well," said Petey, "thank you. Thank you for inviting us. We'll see if we can come. We'll let you know."

"Oh, I can come," Gloria said. "I know I can come."

"You can?" Petey sounded really surprised.

"Yes, Petey," Gloria said firmly, "I can."

Emily smiled. It was probably the first time in Gloria's life that she had made a decision without Petey.

"I have to check home," Petey said. "But I'll come too, if I can." She popped a potato chip into her mouth, chewed it, and then spoke again. "I *want* to come," she said.

Seven

Emily's father had to make two trips to Grandma's house the day of the Hanukkah party. First he dropped off Mother and Lisa. Emily and Sally remained in the car to drive with him while he picked up Simeon, Petey, and Gloria.

Mother ran up the steps to Grandma's house carrying a huge bowl of salad. Emily reminded herself to warn Simeon away from the food prepared in non-kosher kitchens like her own. Lisa stood in the drive for a moment, holding open the car door. "If I had known you were going to invite an army to this party, I'd have brought a few friends along too," she said crossly.

"I think Grandma has enough extra people," Dad said.

"Three for Emily and Sally and none for me?" Lisa retorted. "That's not fair."

"We had to invite them," Emily said. "They needed to come."

"What do you mean, *needed*?"

"Well, Simeon is lonesome, so he needed to come," Emily explained.

"How lonesome are Petey and Gloria?"

"I thought . . ." Emily said slowly. "I thought the party would help them understand."

"Well, I have friends who need to understand too," Lisa said.

"Next year," Dad suggested.

Lisa slammed the door. Dad put the car into gear and steered it down the gravel drive and out onto the road. At Simeon's house, he honked the horn. Simeon's mother opened the door and stood waving to

Simeon as he ran down the walk. Gloria and Petey were both at Petey's house, waiting in the yard. Petey got in front with Sally. Emily shoved over next to Simeon to make room in the back for Gloria. "I'm a little scared," Gloria whispered to Emily.

"Scared? Of what?"

"I've never been to a Jewish thing before," Gloria said. "I won't know how to act."

"It's just a family party," Emily said. "Nothing strange is going to happen. You know some of my relatives. Besides me and Sally, there's Lisa and our parents and Jenny and Jake."

"Well, just don't leave me alone," Gloria said.

"Don't worry. I'll stick to you like we were pasted together. You, me, and Simeon. Sally can stick to Petey."

At Grandma's the five of them sat on the floor in front of the fireplace with Jenny and Jake. Aunt Elsa's grandchildren, Cousin Felice and Cousin James, were there too. They ate chopped liver spread on crackers, drank soda, and eyed the piles of presents growing larger and larger under the picture window at the far end of the room, one pile for each kid. Each group as they arrived put some more brightly wrapped packages on the piles.

Besides Grandma's sisters, Aunt Nan and Aunt Elsa, and Aunt Elsa's husband, Uncle Morty, Jenny and Jake's whole family were there, which included Aunt Lou (Mom's sister), Uncle Andrew, Amy, and Chip. So were Mom's brother, Uncle Larry, and his wife, Aunt Mona, and their two children, Beth and Didi; and Felice and James' parents, Cousins Elaine and Mel. Grandpa's brother, Uncle Alfred, came with his wife, Aunt Millie. His sister, Aunt Etta, walked in with her daughter and son-in-law, Cousins Stacey and Mike. They had two little kids who did nothing for the first half hour after their arrival but run up the stairs in the front hall and slide back down the banister. No one paid any attention to them except their mother, who stood at the foot of the steps, moaning, "Stop, stop."

"I'll never remember all these people," Gloria said.

"You don't have to," Emily said. "Just remember the kids. Lisa. Chip. Amy. Felice. James." She pointed at them as she ticked off their names. "Jake. Jenny. Beth. Didi. Sally. Me. Don't worry about that little boy and girl in the hall. They don't count."

"Do they have names?"

"Yes, but we just call them Terror Tot the First and Terror Tot the Second."

After everyone had hugged, kissed, swallowed a drink, eaten hors d'oeuvres, chatted, and shouted, Grandpa announced that it was time to open the presents. Only the children got presents, small things: caps, mittens, books, crayons, felt-tipped pens, games, little stuffed animals. Aunt Nan's gifts always came in shopping bags, so they each had something in which to lug their loot home. Even Simeon, Gloria, and Petey received gifts. Grandma and Grandpa gave Gloria and Petey each a pair of fancy barrettes, and Simeon a biography of Golda Meir. They received presents from the Berg family too. Emily and Sally had done the shopping: Barbie paper dolls for Petey's and Gloria's collections, two transformers for

Simeon. Emily didn't know whether he collected them or not, but since so many boys did, she thought they were a good bet. He smiled when he opened them and shouted, "Thank you," so she knew she had won.

Dinner was next. The children sat at the table in the kitchen, the grown-ups sat in the dining room. The meal was the same every year—pot roast, tossed salad, green beans, applesauce, and piles and piles of potato pancakes fried in oil. Afterward there'd be chocolate cake baked by Aunt Nan, and fruit salad and coffee and tea.

Emily pointed to the pancakes on Gloria's plate. "You eat these with applesauce," she said. "They're special for the holiday. They're called latkes."

Carefully, Gloria cut a tiny piece of potato pancake with her fork, dipped it into the applesauce, put it into her mouth, and chewed slowly. "It's good," she said. She took a bigger bite. "Delicious."

"Do you want to know why we eat them on Hanukkah?"

Gloria's mouth was full, so she couldn't

reply. Emily explained anyway. "We eat them because they're fried in oil. That's to remind us of the Hanukkah miracle. Two thousand years ago, when the Maccabees rededicated the holy Temple in Jerusalem, they found only enough oil to light the lamp above the ark for one day. But by a miracle, it burned for eight."

Gloria nodded and took another latke off the platter.

After dinner the kids cleared the table. It was growing dark; Grandma closed the blinds in the kitchen and dining room to shut out the night. But she left them open at the picture window in the living room. The menorah, the Hanukkah candleholder, stood on the sill. It was made out of gleaming brass and it had nine branches. One was a little taller than the others. That was for the shammes, the servant candle.

Grandpa recited a prayer: "You are blessed, O Lord our God, King of the Universe, who has made us holy with your commandments, and ordered us to light the Hanukkah lights. You are blessed, O Lord our God, King of the Universe, who performed miracles for our ancestors at this time of the year in olden days."

He lit the shammes, the servant candle. It was the fifth night of Hanukkah, so there were five more candles to light. He gave Grandma the shammes. With it she lit the first candle in the menorah. Then Grandpa, Emily's mother, Aunt Lou, and Uncle Larry lit the other four. Emily liked the eighth night best, when the Hanukkah menorah was ablaze with nine glowing candles. But even six made a pretty good show.

Aunt Nan whispered in Emily's ear. "Round up the others," she said. "It's time to get ready." She moved away from the crowd into the dining room, pulling the sliding doors that separated the two rooms shut behind her.

Emily turned to Gloria. "I have to get ready for our play," she said. "We'll only be gone a few minutes."

"That's okay," Gloria said. She, Petey, and Cousin Felice were playing dominoes. Emily didn't have to worry about leaving them alone for a while. She, Sally, Jenny, Jake, and Simeon ran upstairs to their mothers' old bedroom, now converted into Grandpa's study. They'd brought their stuff over the day before and stored it there. Now they dressed themselves in bathrobes, wrapped Turkish towels around their heads, and seized the swords and shields Jenny had made out of cardboard and aluminum foil.

Back downstairs they slipped into the dining room. With Uncle Andrew's help Aunt Nan had pushed the table and chairs against the rear wall. They'd carried the papier-mâché idol in from the garage through the kitchen and placed it in front of the table. Jenny had copied it from a picture of an ancient statue in the encyclopedia. It was in the shape of a man, with a ferocious face, legs like a lion's, and a funny square beard.

"Boy, he's super," Sally breathed.

"Yes," Jenny agreed. "My masterpiece."

Uncle Andrew returned to the living room. The kids took their places. Aunt Nan opened the doors just wide enough to step through, and then she shut them again. They could no longer see her, but they could hear every word she was saying. "Quiet, please," she shouted. "Quiet, quiet."

Gradually the chatter in the living room died down.

"It's that time," Aunt Nan said, "the time you've all been waiting for."

"Nan is going to do a striptease," someone shouted. Emily recognized Uncle Morty's voice.

"Oh, shut up, Morty," Aunt Nan snapped. She went back to her announcing voice. "It's time for the annual Hanukkah production of the Four Seasons players. This year the Four Seasons decided not to fool around. They are doing the story of the Maccabees, the Hanukkah story itself, in living color and stereophonic sound."

"Yay!" Uncle Morty shouted. A scattering of applause rippled through the room.

"Shhh," Aunt Nan ordered. "As you know, there were five Maccabee brothers. But there are only Four Seasons. So we had to enlist a fifth actor for our production. We are very happy to have Simeon Goldfarb with us today. He will play Simon and a Syrian officer. Sally is Judah Maccabee.

Jenny is John. Jake is the Syrian general and Jonathan. Emily is Matthathias and Eleazar."

"My grandchildren," Grandma said. "Look how many people they can be, all at once."

"Shhh," Aunt Nan ordered again.

"In my own house she tells me to shush," Grandma complained. But she kept quiet.

"And now, ladies and gentlemen," Aunt Nan exclaimed, "the Four Seasons presents *Judah and His Brothers!*" She pushed open the doors and then stepped aside.

The audience gasped. All they could see was the papier-mâché idol. "He's wonderful," Cousin Elaine said. "So scary. Jenny must have made him."

"That's right," said Aunt Lou proudly.

"He looks like my brother-in-law Bernie," said Uncle Morty.

Everyone laughed. "Shhh," Aunt Nan warned yet again.

Jake entered from the kitchen. He stood in front of the idol. The others entered from the hall. Emily faced Jake, her hands on her hips, her legs apart. The others were lined up behind her.

"Mattathias," Jake cried, "you are an important priest of the Jews. The other Jews will do what you do. The King of Syria has conquered Judea. I am his general. I'm in charge here now."

Jenny, Sally, and Simeon hissed. The audience hissed too.

"Quiet!" Jake shouted. His voice was even louder than Aunt Nan's. Everyone shut up instantly. "No harm will come to you," he said, "if you bow down to this statue of the king. If you accept the religion of the Syrians, the king will protect you, and you will live in peace and prosperity. But if you don't, you will die. You and your five sons will all die. If you're stubborn, you'll pay for it. Make up your minds. Bow down to the king. He is god. Or die."

Jake stalked back into the kitchen. Mattathias and his sons talked over the situation. They agreed that they would never bow down to a god made out of stone, or to a human god either. The only god they could worship was the one true God, the God of Israel. They knocked over the idol. They agreed to hide in the mountains and carry on guerrilla warfare against the powerful Syrians. "We don't want to be Greeks or Syrians," Sally said. "We want to be Jews. We have to defend our freedom. We have to defend the religion of Israel and our right to worship as we please."

"We will follow you," Jenny promised. "From now on we will call you Judah Maccabee, Judah the Hammer."

The brothers rushed off. Jake the Syrian general returned. When he saw the idol on the ground, he picked it up. "This is war!" he shouted. "This is war!"

Simeon changed into a different robe and turban, and became a Syrian. He and the Syrian general made laws that oppressed the Jews. They took over God's Temple in Jerusalem, where they set up statues of their king and their other gods. More and more Jews ran off into the hills to join Judah and his brothers. The Syrians had a mighty army. But Judah and his guerrilla fighters

struck at night, unexpectedly. They drove the Syrians crazy.

In a big battle, both Jake and Simeon were killed. Then they slipped out, changed their robes, and came back as Maccabees. Singing, they marched to the Temple in Jerusalem. There they knocked down the idol and stomped on it until it was crushed to bits. The audience cheered.

"Now we must clean this Temple," Sally said. "We must purify it, so that we Jews can again worship God here. Go, Eleazer," she said to Emily. "Go get the special holy oil. We will rekindle the eternal light, and then everyone will know that the holy Temple has been rededicated to God. They will know that the Jews are free once more to follow the faith of their ancestors."

Emily ran off and then ran on again, carrying a little jar. "There's not much oil here," she said. "Only enough for one day. The eternal light will go out again. What should we do?"

"Trust God," said Jenny.

Aunt Nan had put a short, fat candle in

the jar. Sally lit it. They all trooped off into the kitchen. Someone started to applaud. "It's not over yet," Aunt Nan called out.

"Of course not," said Uncle Morty. "It can't be over until we've had the miracle."

The actors trooped on again. "Look!" said Jake. "One whole day has passed, and the oil is still burning."

Again they left their playing area. Again they returned. "Look!" said Simeon. "Two whole days have passed, and the oil is still burning."

Off and on they trooped, six more times. By their eighth return everyone in the audience was reciting with them. "Look! Eight whole days have passed, and the oil is still burning."

"A miracle, a miracle!" cried Sally. "God has made a miracle. And forever afterward, as long as there are Jews, let them celebrate this miracle."

The performers lined up and faced the audience. "The holiday will be called Hanukkah," said Jenny, "because in Hebrew that means 'dedication.' "

"The holiday will last eight days," said Simeon, "because the miracle lasted eight days."

"On the first day, the Jews will light one candle," said Jake. "On the second day they will light two, on the third day three, and so on, until eight candles are burning."

"They will put the menorah with the candles in the window," said Emily. "That way the whole world will see the lights and remember that people should be free to follow their own customs and to worship God as they please."

"THE END," Jake shouted.

The audience broke out into wild applause. The actors bowed. "Encore, encore," Uncle Morty cried.

"There is no more," said Jenny.

"But we can sing," Sally suggested. "We can all sing." In her clear, strong voice, she began a Hanukkah melody.

"Rock of Ages, let our song
     praise Thy saving power."

In a moment all the others had joined in. The music filled the house.

"Thou amidst the raging foe
wast our sheltering tower,
Furious, they assailed us,
but Thine arm availed us,
And Thy word broke their sword
when our own strength failed us."

They sang some other Hanukkah songs too, all the ones they knew. Then Aunt Lou went to the piano and started to play from a book of popular songs. A group gathered around her to sing. Aunt Nan, Simeon, and the Four Seasons cleaned up from the play. They took off their bathrobes. They picked up the pieces of the crushed idol and threw them into the garbage. Jenny put the swords and shields into the front hall so she'd remember to take them home. She was saving them in case they ever needed them for another play. "I wish I could have saved the idol," she mourned. "He was the best."

It was dark now. Some people started to leave. Uncle Larry, Aunt Mona, Beth, and Didi were the first to depart. They lived near Philadelphia, and it would take them two hours to get home.

"We have to go too," Emily's dad announced.

"Why?" Sally asked. She was the only kid at the piano, singing, and she was having a wonderful time.

"Because I'm tired."

"I'm not," Sally said.

"Too bad. But we'll compromise. I'll take your guests home first and then come back for you. Emily can ride with me."

Sally grinned and returned to the piano. Emily rounded up Simeon, Gloria, and Petey. They found Grandma and Grandpa in the front hall, waving good-bye to Terror Tot the First and Terror Tot the Second.

"Thank you very much," Simeon said. "It was nice of you to let us come."

"We had a wonderful time," Gloria said.

"It was very interesting," Petey added. "Thank you for the present."

Grandpa shook their hands. Grandma kissed them each on the cheek. "Perhaps you'll come back at Passover," she suggested, "for the seder."

"Not me," said Simeon. "We go to my grandparents', in Brooklyn."

"Of course," said Grandma. "I mean Petey and Gloria."

"What's the seder?" Petey wanted to know.

"A special service and meal for celebrating Passover," Grandma replied. "Lots of stories, singing, and good food. It lasts half the night."

"It's fun," Emily said. "Actually, I like it better than Hanukkah."

"Me too," Simeon agreed.

"Even though there aren't any presents," Emily added.

"But what's Passover?" Gloria asked.

"It celebrates the Exodus from Egypt, the beginning of the Jewish people," Grandpa explained. "It's a really important holiday."

"More important than Hanukkah?" Petey sounded really surprised. "I thought Hanukkah was like Christmas."

"No," Grandma said. "Christmas is a major Christian holiday; Hanukkah is a minor Jewish holiday. They both have lights in them, and they both happen in December. That's about all they have in common." Petey nodded solemnly.

Emily's dad had pulled up to the front of the house. They exchanged one more set of good-byes, and then the four kids piled into the car. "Listen, Emily," Petey said, "it was super of you to invite us. Really super."

"Yeah," Gloria agreed. "We had a super time."

"And we learned a lot." Petey leaned back in her seat. "We really learned a lot."

In the dark, Emily smiled. It had been a good Hanukkah party. Maybe the best. Maybe the best ever.

Watch Mountain School's Winter Concert always took place the night before school let out for Christmas vacation. This year it was also the eighth night of Hanukkah. On Monday Emily and Sally's wishes had come true. Emily got her ten-speed bike and Sally her little television set. Emily thought it was a really good deal, because of course she'd get the benefit of the TV in their room too. She made up her mind that Sally could borrow the bike whenever she wanted to.

On Tuesday there'd been a Hanukkah party at Hebrew school. Hebrew school parties were pretty boring, but they were better than a regular class. This year the education committee brought in a puppet show. It was something different, anyway.

Before dinner on Wednesday Emily, Sally, Lisa, and their parents lit the twisted Hanukkah candles for the last time that year. Two were red, two were yellow, two were orange, two were blue, and one was white. Nine lights blazed in the window while they sat at the kitchen table and ate. By the time the meal was over, the candles had burned out. Officially, Hanukkah continued until sunset the following day. But for Emily the holiday was over.

They got to school early. The concert was scheduled for seven-thirty, but the kids who were singing had to be there by seven. Sally went off to the fourth-grade room. Emily, Lisa, and their parents found seats in the all-purpose room. Aunt Nan showed up a few minutes later. Then Aunt Lou and Uncle Andrew came in with Jake and Amy. Jake sat down next to Emily. "I don't see Simeon," he said.

"He isn't coming," Emily said. "He won't sing Christmas carols, and he won't listen to them either. That's what he told me."

"I didn't want to come," Jake complained. "Tonight they're showing *Star Trek III* on HBO. But Mom said Jenny was singing, and Sally had a solo, and I had to come. Chip said he had too much homework. She didn't make him come. That's not fair."

Emily sighed. "There's a lot that isn't fair," she said.

The lights dimmed. Mr. Starrett walked up the aisle and sat down at the piano. It had been pushed in front of the platform, so he could conduct the choruses while he played. Mrs. Titus parted the curtains and stepped forward. "Welcome, ladies and gentlemen," she said. "Welcome to Watch Mountain School's annual Winter Concert."

Someone applauded, so then everyone else applauded too. Mr. Starrett began to play "O Come, All Ye Faithful." Grasping candles in foil holders, the students marched in, class by class, singing. Emily felt a thrill down her back. She couldn't help it. The mass of voices, the majestic melody, the pinpricks of light in the darkened room—it was beautiful.

The curtains opened, revealing risers, on which the first graders took their places. The other classes marched up the aisles and out the doors at the front of the room. They would wait their turns in the hall. There wasn't enough space in the all-purpose room for the entire student body and all their relatives and friends.

The classes went in order, from first grade to sixth grade. The kindergartners had had their own program in the afternoon. Each class sang three or four songs, and each class had a soloist or two. You couldn't really hear most of them. But when it was Sally's turn, her rich, powerful tones reached the farthest corners of the room:

"Long lay the world in sin and error
  pining,
Till He appeared and the soul felt its
  worth. . . ."

"Fall on your knees!" sang the rest of the class. "O hear the angel voices. . . ."

Sally had an angel voice. Emily knew it. Everyone else knew it too. Emily and her family applauded so hard after "O Holy Night" that their palms turned red. So did all the other people in the room.

The fourth grade disappeared after their songs. They had returned to the classroom. Emily knew Mrs. Glendenning had bought ice cream and cookies for them to eat while they were waiting to come back at the end, when all the students and the audience would sing "Silent Night" together. "Too bad," Emily whispered to Jake. "Too bad I'm not getting any of the ice cream and cookies."

She wondered if next year she'd fight another battle in her Christmas revolution. Simeon would be off at his live-in yeshiva, and a person could never tell in advance what sort of notion Jake would take into his head.

She knew she wouldn't enjoy sitting in the library alone. She might give in. She'd sung carols in the past; she might do it again. She couldn't be sure.

She realized her Christmas problem had no solution. The world wasn't going to stop celebrating Christmas. Why should the world do any such thing? On the other hand, the holiday wasn't going to stop making her uncomfortable.

But at that moment, sitting in the all-purpose room of Watch Mountain School, Emily was content. She and Sally and Petey and Gloria were friends again. Simeon wasn't Mr. Popularity, but at least he was no longer blamed for something he hadn't done. Hanukkah had been super, with a wonderful family party, a bearable Hebrew school celebration, and a ten-speed bike. She'd worry about next year when next year came.

ABOUT THE AUTHOR

BARBARA COHEN wrote many popular books for children, including *The Carp in the Bathtub*, which critics have described as a modern classic. Her other books include *Tell Us Your Secret, The Long Way Home, The Orphan Game,* and *Molly's Pilgrim.*